THE DEVOTED OF JASIREY

Haley's
Athol, Massachusetts

Haley's
488 South Main Street
Athol, MA 01331
marcia2gagliardi@gmail.com • 978.249.9400

Copy edited by Phillis Scott with editorial consultation.

Cover by Elizabeth Lindgren.

International Standard Book Number: 978-1-956055-31-3
Library of Congress Number: pending

for Jack,
my real-life teddy bear
and
steadfast supporter

All people are caught in an inescapable network of mutuality,
tied in a single garment of destiny.

—Martin Luther King, Jr.

Do not be afraid. Our fate cannot be taken from us. It is a gift.

—Dante Alighieri

Contents

Preparing for Jasirey

Ian positioned his team in a narrow refuse-strewn lane built during the days when foot traffic predominated in Bambari, a small city in the Central African Republic. A lone bony mutt slunk from one worn brick building to another. Nostrils flaring, the dog snuffled through litter and lifted its snout every few feet. Ian wished he carried a dog biscuit.

Amador, earrings chiming, passed close enough to the shadowed wall Ian leaned against for him to see the tear-shaped beads of perspiration pearling along the edges of her cropped hair. Her hips swayed to a muted bass beat spilling from someone's open window. The team's sniper Lee had set up his rifle on the rooftop across from the targeted building and signaled his readiness.

Two men, T-shirts stretched over their chests and arms, stepped from the doorway, fondling semiautomatic weapons. Amador's torso inched toward them, though her feet remained planted.

They spoke crude, Russian-accented French. "Prostituée? Entrez, ma belle."

Amador blew a kiss and watched the men crumple at her feet. "Nice shots," she said to the other two members of the team. She retrieved the tranq darts from the guards' necks.

Fael and Liu dragged the pair to a dark alley. Humming, Amador resumed her act and confidently entered the building into a short, empty hallway smelling of mildew. She signaled the others and stood aside for the men to move past her. One door sat on each side of the hallway.

Tranq gun in hand, Ian tested the left door . . . unlocked. He slipped through, and Fael followed suit through the right. He left the small forms huddled on the floor to Liu and Amador and darted two adults lying like lumps on cots along a wall.

Amador and Liu jumped when Fael's burnous flicked their legs as he whirled to grab a boot-shod foot shooting past his ribs. He tugged sharply and slammed a jab into the arm hurtling toward his gut. A long knife skittered across the floor.

Arm wrapped about the assailant's neck, Fael choked off her curse in Russian and folded straight down, his legs pinning her arms. He dug into pressure points on her neck until she lost consciousness and then shoved her limp body aside to grab the knife.

Liu switched on his penlight, caught Fael's gleaming eyes, and stepped in front of the incapacitated woman.

"She can identify us," whispered Fael, staring at the downed woman.

Liu shrugged. "We have spoiled Marcus's plans before. It is unlikely he will announce his own involvement in buying these children for his trafficking ring by reporting us to the constabulary."

Ian joined them. "Two down next door." He held out a hand to Fael and gave a casual nod when the knife lay in his palm. "How are the children?"

Five pairs of thin arms clutched at one another. Fael's eyes cooled. "You are safe, little ones," he said in French. A girl, perhaps six, eyes shimmering, raised her arms. Fael curled the child into his chest.

Amador repeated Fael's words in the children's native Sango. "I know a couple who can be trusted to care for these children," she said to Ian. "Liu and I can get them there on foot."

"Good," Ian said.

Liu, the team's healer, took the child Fael held. "I shall examine the children when we are safe," he said.

"Join us at the campsite as soon as you can," Ian said. "The sun rises in six hours. We need to leave before then."

❧ ❧ ❧

Five miles outside the city, deep in the savanna, three shelter tents rose in minutes after Liu and Amador arrived. A small fire hidden amidst the tall grass and scrubby acacia trees, sufficient to deter four-legged predators, flickered with the force of Lee's sigh.

Amador patted his bicep, as big around as coconuts on the island of the Devoted. "I am sorry I was unable to find more accurate information, Lee.

His broad cheeks dimpled. "Not your fault the wise woman was too old for our purpose.

"I have been a recruiter for twelve years," Amador said, "and have recommended twice that many people to be interviewed as possible members of the Devoted. But, when I heard people in Bambari praising her mediation skills and uncanny advice on which crops to plant based on her predictions of dry or wet years, for the first time I recommended someone to be interviewed as a potential candidate for our Jasirey. Perhaps I allowed my excitement to cloud my judgment."

"I think not," Liu said. "You reported the information about the wise woman, and as the ruling body regarding searches for Jasirey, the Imperiat decided to send a team to investigate."

"You followed protocol," Fael said. "Each Devoted team has the same mission to aid victims of natural or manmade disasters in preparation for our lady's work."

Lee continued the mantra. "To search for her—Jasirey, a woman destined to sow seeds of stability in a precarious world."

"While remaining in the background, unrecognized," Liu said.

"Vowing to serve Jasirey on her destined path," Amador finished.

"Our being in the Republic," Ian said, "saved the time needed for another team to get here after Amador heard the rumors of someone called the bleached man collecting children. They may not have gotten here in time to stop Marcus. Having run up against him before, we recognized the description, quickly found the children's location, and could stop him: a good day's work, I'd say."

No one argued.

"Get some sleep," Ian told them. "We leave before first light."

❧ ❧ ❧

On the jolting drive back to Bambari, Amador, the team's designated driver, removed her swinging earrings one-handed and flashed a grin at Ian sitting in the front passenger seat. "The Republic has few resources to spare on infrastructure."

Ian nodded and, as the open-sided truck hit another rut, wedged his boot against the gearbox. "Liu, report on the children," he said, hoping for a distraction from his aching muscles.

Liu raised his voice above the rattling din. "Malnourished, the usual parasites, nothing critical. I left medicines and instructions with the foster couple, a decent sort."

"I set up a Devoted contact," Amador said, "to help supply the children's needs." Assigned to the Central African Republic for some time, she well knew its people's hardships.

Amador delivered the men to a small, battered plane that blended in with local aircraft parked near one of Bambari's grass-covered airstrips.

"Gentlemen, nice working with you," she said.

Lee winked. "Come back to the island soon for a visit."

The men jumped down from the truck. Amador gave them a two-fingered salute and drove away.

Ian set course for Hurghada, a major Egyptian Red Sea tourist attraction where his private jet waited at the Hurghada International Airport. The larger plane would provide amenities needed for the long flight to the island of the Devoted.

Strictly for the tourist trade and a good place for a disparate group to blend in, the resort contained no settlements of locals.

Ian also needed to report Marcus's activities to the Devoted hub of African operatives located at El Dathar, an old town bazaar.

❧ ❧ ❧

Marcus's temper rose with the God-awful heat as he batted away another swirl of grit rising from the rudimentary track winding inland through the savanna. The Central African Republic might be a country of higher elevation, but it still got bloody hot. He again wiped under his safari hat and wraparound sunglasses, then flung the sodden handkerchief out of the open-sided vehicle. Hot-wired by Strafe, Marcus's do-anything man, the rust bucket at least attracted no one's attention.

The operation had been compromised, and Strafe immediately contacted the pilot to route Marcus's jet, a hawk among the local sparrows at Bambari's airfield, to an airstrip across the border into Cameroon. When the two men reached the plane and after a quick flight to Bonny on the neighboring Nigerian coast where several commodities awaited them, they would return to Douala, the port of Cameroon, and Marcus's merchantman.

To Marcus, the loss of commodities in the Republic meant a few substandard orphans lost a chance at regular meals and shelter, which caused nary a ripple in the ocean of the poverty-stricken. Marcus had intended their quick sale as laborers. Even slovenly sex shops occasionally cleaned their sheets and toilets—whether indoor plumbing, outhouses, or pots.

He carried the Republic's best asset—diamonds acquired through an independent miner—nestled in a velvet pouch tucked into the spine of his briefcase. "I wonder," Marcus said, "what brought Ian and his merry band to the Republic?"

Strafe snorted. "The informants were slow. I recognized the description of the mountain and his Mini-Me immediately."

Marcus knew from his mercenaries' reports the two men to whom Strafe referred—a large Polynesian and a spare, lithe Arab. He frowned at the jealousy in Strafe's tone. Preferring that his people never become complacent while in his service, Marcus fostered competitiveness among them but not with outsiders. Such competition could prove a fatal distraction.

Strafe, bought from an uncle burdened with the child's care, showed intelligence and adaptability beyond the ordinary. Marcus sent Strafe at age sixteen, forged identity papers in hand, to Germany to a school specializing in computer coding, in which he excelled.

Strafe found hacking computer codes stimulating, and his work for Marcus kept him in beer and chips, vintage motorcycles, and young pussy. Most important to Marcus was Strafe's invincible loyalty, instilled step by painstaking step, year by year—Marcus's greatest achievement among all the children who passed his stringent training protocols. He sent the others, all credits to his business reputation, into the world to earn their way. Strafe served no one save Marcus.

"Whoever they work for," Strafe said, "Ian and his team never mention an organizational name. I've tried facial recognition. They're not in the system."

Strafe stated a simple fact. He was not making excuses for his failure, so Marcus accepted the situation and, though it pained him, dismissed the younger man's grammatical error of whoever instead of whomever.

Marcus's mercenaries had encountered Ian's group in other countries while scouting for commodities. They knew Ian's name because they had traced him to America. What rankled Marcus most were the personal inconvenience and precious loss of time. Ian rose on the scale from occasional annoyance to decided nuisance, one he intended to eliminate. Every man had his vices, secret passions, or plain everyday loved ones he would compromise himself to protect.

"Concentrate on Ian," Marcus said. "I want to know where he goes, what he does."

✻ ✻ ✻

Arriving in the evening twilight, Ian's team folded themselves into a cab and went to the middling hotel where Fael had made reservations.

In the morning, the team ate breakfast on the balcony of Ian's room. Liu plucked purple grapes from a small cluster, his eyes riveted on the bright reds, yellows, and greens of windsurfers' sails. He winced then laughed when one wobbled and hit the deep-blue water like a flapping sea bird.

Lee pushed a pancake into his mouth and scowled at Fael's smirk. "What? They're mouth-sized." He held up a second pancake to demonstrate.

"Your mouth, perhaps."

Ignoring his teammates' banter, Liu said, "I suggest we walk to the bazaar for exercise."

Everyone agreed and, carrying small packs, soon set out for El Dathar. The team mingled with the crowd and stopped at stalls selling food—from cassava to make tapioca to cooked kebabs—and crafts from handwoven rugs to beaten metal pots and pans.

At a wood carver's stall when no other shoppers stood nearby, Fael—the only team member who spoke Arabic—slipped through a tent flap behind the vendor.

He returned in ten minutes and nodded that the report had been given. The men casually continued through the bazaar, then hailed a cab to take them to the airport.

✻ ✻ ✻

Nine time zones later, Ian landed the jet on the one hard-packed earth runway on the island of the Devoted and handed the craft over to the ground crew. He ordered Fael and Lee to report to the Imperiat, the ruling body charged with missions directly related to Jasirey.

He sprinted to the security center hidden within the cone of the dead volcano that had spawned the island. Master Kai, head of the Imperiat, waited for him. The man who had mentored Ian through his

6

induction into the Devoted had changed little since Ian met him while in college.

Master Kai sat on a cushion before a low table in a small office and poured oolong from an unadorned white teapot into handleless cups.

Ian bowed and sat across from the older man.

"I shall keep this meeting short," Master Kai said. "You are due in Vermont, yes?"

I am," Ian said. "It's good to see you, sir."

Master Kai lifted his hand in a short wave. "Proceed with your report. We shall speak of more personal matters afterward."

Ian recounted meeting the wise woman too elderly to be a candidate for Jasirey and freeing the children from sex slavery. "In my judgment, the risk of the locals discovering our involvement was minimal. We didn't encounter Marcus, the trafficker. The team sent to the country by the Hurghada hub reported losing his trail in Cameroon."

"Clever," Master Kai said. "A more populated country and therefore an easier place to lose oneself. A coast—ports—where he has no doubt anchored his merchantman."

Ian's mouth thinned. "He'll have less to transport now."

"Yes." Master Kai rose easily, belying his age. "Excuse me a moment. I wish to send a message to the council before it leaves my mind." He crossed to a small desk and opened a laptop.

Ian knew many of the council members. They governed Devoted business interests throughout the world—often intersecting with the corporation he owned—and missions not directly related to Jasirey.

Ian checked his mental to-do list: a stopover in Boston to pick up his American business clothes and to call Charlotte—despite knowing it would annoy his efficient admin—to check that his private cottage at the Vermont resort chosen to host the training seminar had been rented. Not usually involved in trainings, Ian was particularly interested in their new research lab sponsored by the Devoted.

The lab would study the efficacy of current methods used to prevent more land from being turned into desert, how to mitigate flooding and sandstorms caused by land already denuded of trees and brush, and the possibility of using satellites to track the temperature of land areas used for agriculture or grazing. It fascinated him that rising land temperatures might indicate a coming drought and give those using the land a heads-up on where sustainable grass could be grazed or when drought-resistant crops should be planted.

Master Kai returned to his seat and regarded Ian with a steady concentration the younger man always found unnerving. Ian felt pulled into the orbit of those dark eyes and came back to himself with no idea how much time had passed.

Master Kai's eyes crinkled with age and humor. "I believe you shall find the coming days quite interesting."

Ian shivered.

Lonely Hearts

Though mid-February in Vermont, the mountains lay bare, no storms forecasted. *A stagnant lull for the ski lodges,* Shannon supposed, *or the harder work of manufacturing decent runs—white strips bandaging the scraped mountain passes.* Home, western Massachusetts, rolled and dipped in less dramatic waves. Entering the final leg of their trip, Shannon drove close to the middle of a narrow switchback. Pine trees speared above the steep edges and cast waning shadows on the road that several times startled her foot to the minivan's brake.

"Glad I'm not driving," Lizzie said.

Shannon risked a glance at her friend's white, pinched mouth. She exhaled a deep breath as the road leveled and opened to the resort's long line of cookie-cutter, two-apartment cottages perched over the valley far below.

She parked at their assigned cottage and knew better than to offer Lizzie a hand climbing down. Shannon slid out and rose on tiptoe, arms stretched overhead. Lizzie's cramped gait shouted pain, and she glared at the steps cut into the winter-withered bank leading to their bottom apartment.

Shannon lifted the hatch of Lizzie's van to suitcases and bulging travel bags jammed into every available air pocket. Shannon's compact suitcase and cooler sat on the back bench seat. She handed Lizzie the apartment key card and one bag, then twined the handles of four heavier bags between her own fingers. Lizzie leaned heavily on the steps' rough-hewn handrail. At the bottom, trembling in the frigid air, she swiped three times before the door unlatched in sync with the dot of green light.

They passed through a small mudroom to the living room where Lizzie dropped her bag onto the durable carpet. "Nicer than my first apartment—and a fireplace." She limped down the hall to peek into the bedrooms and back. "You take the master, Shan."

9

Shannon studied her friend's jutting chin. "Let's flip a coin."

"I said I'll take the smaller one."

Shannon gave Lizzie's shoulders a light rub. "I didn't know about the stairs."

Lizzie let her head rest on Shannon's shoulder for two seconds, then toed the bags on the floor. "If I empty these, you can put stuff in them, make the coolers lighter."

"We'll see. I know my limits."

Thankful the landing-sized steps lessened the steep climb, Shannon returned to the van, worked Lizzie's cooler past the bumper, and stepped back into a solid mass. Long arms shot past her to guide the cooler to the ground.

"May I be of assistance?"

Shannon tilted her head back to flash an apologetic smile at the trod-on man. Bareheaded, he had neither hat nor hair to cover it. The blank canvas emphasized heavy lidded eyes so dark they reflected the lowering sun along with male amusement.

"I'm in the top apartment. Ian." He held out a hand, his fingers overlapping her wrist.

"Shannon," she said as she indicated the hatch. "Afraid we over-packed. I'd be grateful for the help."

"No problem." Ian hefted the cooler. Shannon winced at his mut-ed grunt.

In the apartment, Lizzie launched into instant familiarity. "We drove up from Massachusetts. Another friend of Shannon's donated this time-share to us, and Shan left her sons with her ex to help me take care of my husband's last wishes."

"I'm sorry for your loss," Ian said.

Lizzie's eyes glistened, but she firmed her trembling lip and directed him to set the coolers outside the kitchenette.

Shannon knew that placing the coolers inside would block the doors of the stove and refrigerator, amenities she counted on to save them money on meals.

"Are you from Vermont, Ian?" Shannon asked.

"No. Boston. Here on business."

After the pair emptied the van, Lizzie searched through her cavernous purse. She bristled at Shannon's head shake. "Fine." The wallet flounced back into the purse. "Thanks for the help, Ian. Why don't you let us pay you back with dinner tonight?" Behind her back, Lizzie pointed her middle finger at her scolding friend.

Lips twitching, Shannon glanced at Ian. She sensed no uneasiness at Lizzie's abrupt invitation and said, "We brought plenty if you care to bring someone."

"As . . . manager, I'm staying alone in the apartment. I'd appreciate the company."

"Is there a conference center here?"

"We rented one of the resort's townhouses for lodging the instructors and trainees and holding trainings—less expensive than a hotel and nicer when it's time to relax."

Those ultra-luxurious houses sat high on the mountain. Shannon assumed that Ian stayed at a separate residence to maintain a professional distance.

"I'll leave you to settle in," he said, "and see you at dinner."

The door closed, and Lizzie said, "Nice guy but funny-looking."

"Interesting, large hands," Shannon said. "Pretty guys look bland to me." She rolled her eyes at the gleam in Lizzie's. "I'm sure he has someone."

Lizzie sighed. "Maybe that moral autopilot of yours is right and it's too soon for your boys to see you dating, but what they don't know won't hurt you. A girl needs a little fun."

❧ ❧ ❧

Ian set up his laptop in the dining alcove, a duplicate of the one downstairs. He had reports to sift through on the efficacy of measures being used to stop desertification and/or sandstorms—planting trees and ground cover to keep water and wind from stripping away topsoil from cleared lands and ways to make sustainable agriculture profitable for poorer regions unable to afford more modern methods.

Unfortunately, eyes the color of blue spruce trees and a small face framed by prematurely white, pixyish hair occupied his mind. While shaking Shannon's hand, Ian had felt a sparking current race up his arm that then morphed into such an intense feeling of connection it had unsettled—and intrigued—him.

11

Not having so much lost hope of a wife and family as having become comfortable in his bachelor state, Ian felt those longings simmer back to the surface.

❧ ❧ ❧

Shannon recognized the expensive label on the bottle of wine Ian brought with him and floundered for a polite way around her predicament. Lizzie couldn't be bothered.

"My medications and alcohol don't mix. Miss Teetotaler only drinks tea."

For once appreciating Lizzie's lack of filters, Shannon said, "The better the wine, the more it tastes like vinegar to me. Can't get past the nasty smell of stronger alcohol."

Ian's laugh lines creased. "I ought to have brought chocolates. I've never known a woman to scorn them."

"Because we're smart," Lizzie said.

Ian exaggerated a prolonged sniff at the already laid table. "Reminds me of my mother's crust—melted in your mouth—and the gravy she served at family dinners."

Shannon lit up at his appreciation. "Chicken pot pie. I had fun cooking and freezing meals for this vacation. My two teenage sons prefer prepackaged food to homemade these days."

"You have kids?" Lizzie asked Ian.

"No, I never married."

Lizzie served herself and pushed aside the carrots and onions from the potpie. "My husband . . . Bobby. We have a girl and a boy, dumb as rocks, but my grandchildren are brilliant." She flicked a hand at Shannon's wince. "You won't think yours are so great in another couple of years either. We did have fun, though, when they were kids. Shannon used to come over with her guitar before she got married, and we'd sing along at the picnic table. I miss those days."

After Ian finished two helpings, Shannon fetched the granola cookies she'd baked and ice cream. Lizzie pushed away her half-filled plate and ate two of the palm-sized cookies.

She batted her eyes at Ian. "We're going to the fitness center tomorrow. Want to come along and eat here? We brought enough to feed an army."

"Dinner in the company of two diverting ladies sounds good. I can drive us to the center after trainings if you like." Lizzie agreed and yawned several times. Ian took his cue from Shannon's concerned glances and wished the women a good night.

❧ ❧ ❧

The dynamics between Shannon and Lizzie reminded Ian of Lee, Liu, and Fael. The time difference worked out, so he Skyped, finding them at the security center.

"Any news on Marcus?" he asked.

"None," Fael said, "and as we expected, no sign of his ship."

Lee dismissed business with a sly smile. "So, training at a ski resort. Met any ski bunnies?"

Fael sighed. Lee admired American phraseology. He doubted his friend always understood their entire sense.

"My neighbors, two lovely ladies, invited me to dinner." Ian waited a beat for interest to pique. "One, the divorced mother of two, the other recently widowed."

Lee gave a scoffing growl. "Time to stop shoving your dream of a family to the back burner. Start cooking."

"Mm, take your own advice," Ian said.

Lee grinned. "I'm content to wait for Jasirey."

"Perhaps it is fortunate Amador is assigned to Africa." Fael ducked Lee's mock roundhouse and, in a more serious vein, said to Ian, "These women concern you."

Ian rubbed over his scalp. Fael had infallible radar. "Shannon, the divorced one, lets her friend do most of the talking. Shy, I think, caregiver sort."

Fael's raised brow silently prompted Ian.

"She's middle-aged. Her kids are teenagers. Doubt she'd want more."

Lee again leaned forward. "No harm in getting acquainted. Any woman your age is bound to have had a marriage or two. Don't want to be a daddy to your bride, do you?" He laughed at Ian's grimace.

❧ ❧ ❧

In the morning at the resort's on-site bakery, Lizzie envied Shannon as she homed in on a display of sticky buns. The abundance of goodies confounded Lizzie, and the sterile, bright white light spilling from cases crowding both sides of a narrow aisle gave her the heebie-jeebies. They reminded her of a hospital.

Hospitals pressed choices on loved ones and patients alike. Bobby's stem cell transplant failed. The cancer returned, and he contracted pneumonia. Bobby's living will clearly stated he wanted no life support machines and no resuscitation. She fought the emergency doctor's decision to put him on a ventilator and now had to wonder if his death were her fault.

Nitpicky details—the funeral, paperwork, insurance, paperwork, the will, paperwork—Lizzie's burdened brain railed. She refused to dwell on the heavy plastic box wrapped in Bobby's favorite plaid shirt, a surprisingly small box for a man who still loomed large. Releasing his ashes would again spear her with having lost him.

Lizzie shot questions at the bakery clerk and shook off Shannon's appeasing hand. There should be descriptive labels. The clerk wore a tolerant smile as part of her uniform. *I'd like to wipe the smile off that patronizing bitch's face*, Lizzie thought. But after a series of taste tests, she chose a confection between strawberry shortcake and a Napoleon.

Shannon drove them to the historic town in the valley. White clapboard buildings with mullioned windows preserved the feel of the colonial era. "Okay, kid?" she asked Lizzie.

"Bobby won't ever be again."

"Neither of us believes that."

Lizzie sulked but followed Shannon into a shop filled with Americana, her favorite decor. Ignoring the raised tourist's price, Lizzie bought a wedding-ring quilt in gingham shades of blue. Down a side street, they found metal figures ranging from two palm-sized deer, antlers locked, to waist-high children, faces alight with glee and hands linked in the childhood game of whip.

Frozen in the moment, they were spared the danger of losing their grip.

❦ ❦ ❦

After his training session and before dinner, Ian drove the women to the fitness center. Shannon imagined the glug, glug, glug of gas at every tap of the SUV's gas pedal. Few lingered at exercises. The dinner hour had started at the elegant and pricey restaurant in the main lodge. After changing into her suit, Lizzie rejected the chillier indoor pool for the hot tub—out in the open air but no more than twenty feet from the building.

Shannon swam to the pool's edge to begin an exercise routine. Ian asked her to teach him, and she demonstrated movements that used the water as resistance. His long arms swooping in and out of the water reminded Shannon of an eagle skimming a river for fish.

"You'd make a good trainer," he said, "—precise instructions and patience."

She smiled. "You get better resistance using pool noodles."

Ian decided that deflecting his compliment spoke to her unaffected, straightforward personality rather than an issue of self-esteem. His hand froze mid lift to brush away water drops from her cheeks. He swam to the stairs.

Together, they went outside and skittered barefoot over platter-sized flagstones to the hot tub where Lizzie luxuriated alone. Shannon stared up at the glittering sky, its lights undimmed by manmade competition. Ian stared at her face glowing with wondrous awe.

Back at the apartment, Lizzie asked him to build a fire. They sat down to spaghetti and meatballs, a meal Ian remembered fondly from childhood but, during his adult years, had traded for more sophisticated fare. Popping in a wound forkful, he wondered why as tomatoes, garlic, and peppers burst on his tongue. He and Shannon continued eating when, after a few mouthfuls, Lizzie excused herself to place the call she'd been dreading.

One of Bobby's buddies owned several acres in Vermont he kept for hunting. Bob had asked him to allow Lizzie to release his ashes there. Having to honor the request scarcely three months later had sent the man reeling. He dictated directions and planned to meet the women midmorning the next day.

Lizzie hung up and tidied the kitchen, pots clanging and dishes rattling as she regained her composure. At home, she hugged her husband's pillow, praying for a sense of his presence. The loss of a partner hit hard enough, but the loss of a shared life almost hit harder. At his insistence and despite her disabling rheumatoid arthritis, she had handled Bobby's physical care. Everything in the past three years had revolved around her husband. She hadn't a clue how to create a life alone.

Shannon said to Ian, "Please don't be offended if I ask you to leave."

"Not a problem." He gave Lizzie a bolstering squeeze. "I'll keep you in my prayers."

"Yeah. Good. Thanks."

Lizzie puttered, paced, decided she needed air, and dragged Shannon outside.

"I can't take this." Lizzie's breath chugged in white puffs. "What kind of life . . ." Her flat palm tapped a rapid tattoo on her chest. ". . . without your heart?" White vapor streamed out. "He could act like a jerk, selfish-guy stuff, but I loved him."

"And he, you," Shannon said. "Roger loved being married. To whom didn't matter particularly. Hell, after the birth of the boys, I never even got laid."

Lizzie snorted at the unexpected crudeness.

Shannon smiled as Lizzie's tight posture eased and said, "Few fights or disagreements—and less sex in two decades of marriage than most people have in their first year of coupledom."

"Coupledom—I like that. But no question you were deprived."

"I vowed for better or worse so stayed in a dead marriage. Not sure it was ever alive." Shannon shrugged. "Truthfully, the kids and finances kept me anchored for a long time. We tried therapy."

Shannon gave a deadpan delivery of advice she had often read in self-help books. "'No one else can make you happy.' Relationships should come with contracts, spell out expectations and obligations. I felt like my grandmother's china and embroidered linens left in the hope chest, unappreciated and buried under unfulfilled promises."

"I'm no fan of divorce, but, honestly, I think Roger wanted a mother more than a wife. You deserve the same kind of passion Bobby and I shared."

"Even if the boys were ready, I have zero interest in complicating our lives with another relationship. I'm happy to concentrate on myself and my sons."

Lizzie grabbed Shannon's hand. "My dreams are dead, but I still get to dream for you."

❦ ❦ ❦

Bobby's friend had mowed a path through a meadow bordered by pines and ending at a solitary apple tree.

Lizzie shook in the freezing air and sobbed as she spread each cupful of ashes. "I'm doing it, Bobby. I'm doing what you wanted."

Bobby once confided to Shannon that he seldom shot at anything on his hunting trips. He sat in a blind, vegged out to the peaceful quiet of the woods, and ate the junk food his strict wife banned at home. He watched, open-mouthed, when a magnificently antlered deer walked past his hideout, the highlight of his hunting career. Beer and tall stories with the guys didn't suck either.

The sun's rays filtering through the pines to highlight the apple tree and huge hoofprints preserved in a mud patch near where a deer had wallowed made the perfect memorial.

Returning to the resort midafternoon, Lizzie soaked in the tub as much for comfort as pain relief and headed straight to bed. Shannon swallowed two ibuprofen tablets and continued working on an afghan she was crocheting for her younger son.

Ian knocked a few hours later and offered blue daisies surrounding a wide sparkling silver candle. Lizzie favored glitter on clothes, shoes, bags, and more. Shannon found it sweet he'd noticed.

"Lizzie's resting?"

"Done for the night, I think. It was difficult."

Ian placed the candle on the dining room table and checked out the afghan spread on the sofa. An old-fashioned train depicted in the stitches billowed steam past snowcapped mountains.

"Amazing detail," he said.

"My son Michael started a love affair with trains as a toddler." Shannon turned toward the kitchen. "Would you like some dessert and tea?"

Recognizing that simple politeness drove the invitation, Ian declined. "Tomorrow, I'm working through dinner. The day after, I'd be happy to chauffer you and Lizzie around town if she feels up to it."

The weird notion occurred to Shannon that he'd rearranged his schedule to extend the invitation. Silly.

❧ ❧ ❧

Marcus sat down for a late supper aboard his well-appointed merchantman. He preferred to eat in his stateroom in the company of three dogs he'd rescued from the fights. Marcus fed and trained them. Their loyalty belonged to him.

The room, spare of clutter, contained serviceable furniture and Marcus's one indulgence, an antique desk he'd restored from a horrendous coat of dark paint some fool had slapped on the light oak. Wood, strong and malleable, lent itself to whatever form one pressed upon it. The patina of a well-used piece enhanced its beauty. Metal, though cold and lifeless, provided strength. Plastic he despised for the foul chemicals he swore he smelled, even tasted.

Ordered to Marcus's stateroom, Strafe entered without knocking. "Ian's back in the States," he said, "at a resort in Vermont. No trace again of the big guy, his Mini-Me, or their Asian tag-along." He sat at the desk, wary eyes roaming over the calm but watchful dogs. "Got the process started on replacing the people we lost." Marcus knew the frequent turnover of mercenaries vexed Strafe, but no one second-guessed his dictates.

❧ ❧ ❧

Only a few weeks in Marcus's hands had made it clear to Strafe that pleasing Marcus determined whether life was worth living, was one of mean drudgery, or soon ended in death for those who refused to adapt. Young enough and attractive once fattened up, Strafe had been earmarked for the sex trade.

He took one look, he remembered, at a bench full of instruments meant to accustom his tender rump to stretching and bit the hand forcing him to lie across the bench. He saw his own teeth marks fly at his head and wound up on the floor, confused between spots on the carpet and blacker floating dots. An icy guttural command stopped the foot aimed at his ribs, and the trainer landed beside Strafe. Meaty hands hauled Strafe to his feet.

"Now, what is all this?" the man said in English, a language Strafe understood somewhat. He trembled mutely before the man. Words never helped against adults.

"Listen, child, do you not want to live well? To have things that will make you happy?"

Strafe's puzzled little face made the man smile.

"Give pleasure to others, and they will reward you with good food, sweets, clothes, and toys." The man's benign expression registered surprise at Strafe's unexpectedly adult grimace. "You have something else you would prefer?"

Strafe's hands clenched and unclenched as he bounced up and down on his toes. He blurted, "I want to learn computers." He had seen a social worker using one once.

The man cocked his head. "Do you? Well, then, let us strike a bargain. You give your best at this training, and you will also be taught computer science. Deal?"

Strafe, expecting another adult lie, reluctantly shook the man's extended hand. Amazing to him, the morning started with instructions on accessing the internet. Strafe was hooked. He endured the sore throats, occasional bloody stools, and deliberately inflicted pain that left no marks by the more brutal trainers. One time, he needed the medic. That trainer disappeared.

After several weeks, Strafe noticed that other children—"Marcus's elite," the guards sneered—began to receive new clothes and be taken away. His computer classes extended to lunch and then past lunch until one day Marcus sent for him.

"Strafe will be the name you use on the computer," Marcus said. "Your teacher tells me you have a natural aptitude for coding. Work hard, and you will be of great value to me."

Unable to sit for a week after gloating over his good fortune to another child, one of Strafe's few mistakes, he soon learned what Marcus expected and what he did and did not tolerate. Strafe—he no longer remembered any other name—owed much to Marcus and gladly gave his best in anything asked of him.

Marcus's odd raptor eyes glistened in the light from the merchantman's porthole. "Book a flight to Vermont. Ferret out Ian's weak spots."

❧ ❧ ❧

The day of Shannon, Lizzie, and Ian's excursion dawned with an eye-searing brightness and a skin-parching cold wind. Shannon slid her sunglasses back on inside a glassblower's shop to study a window display floodlighted by the sun. Raised veins, bumps, and swells in pulsing reds and yellows streaked into fluorescent orange on heavy, shield-sized decorative plates. Shannon hid a shudder.

An interior viewing window allowed patrons to watch the artisans. The skill required to shape larger items at the end of the blowing tube and simultaneously integrate colors and textures fascinated Shannon. In the display room, a vase in swirls of amethyst, sapphire, and emerald drew her attention. Had she the means, she'd collect that type of blown glass.

"This piece attracts you," Ian said.

"I imagine it holding lilacs and daffodils."

"Pretty. Will you buy it?"

Shannon shook her head.

Ian realized the women managed on restricted budgets. "Would you mind if I do?"

"Of course not. For your girlfriend?"

Ian detected no guile in her eyes or body language. "No girlfriend at the moment."

"Sorry. Was that prying? Sometimes the line blurs for me."

Ian forced a light tone. "Feel free to ask me anything."

Taste-testing took up the better part of the next stop with horse-radish and garlic-herb cheeses, nut butters, and mango and blueberry chutneys. The taste of Macintosh apple lingered on the tongue from a complimentary cup of cider.

Lizzie made a second circuit. "Lunch," she said.

By late morning, Lizzie's gait deteriorated to an unable-to-walk-a-straight-line shamble, and Shannon suggested returning to the resort. Ian supported Lizzie on the way to the car.

"Shall I drive you to the fitness center later?" he asked as he parked at their cottage.

"Shannon," Lizzie said, "why be stuck here all afternoon listening to me snore? Go have fun. Just pick me up before you go to the pool. Maybe we can have dinner out." She nudged Ian. "Use your persuasive charms, bub. She thinks you're cute."

Ian's breath hitched, and Shannon sighed.

Lizzie whispered to Shannon. "You said it—large hands, interesting. Please."

Reduced to a squirming adolescent asking the woman of his dreams for a date, Ian said to Shannon. "Any idea where you'd like to go?"

Shannon picked a one-room art gallery tucked into a grove of birch trees. She preferred oil-painted landscapes and paused before a canvas showing a weathered covered bridge dappled with bronze and russet leaves. "I envy artists. Paint-by-number kits are the best I can do."

"Ever try art lessons?"

"I've learned my limitations—no talent for drawing. I just follow directions well. What's your creative outlet? Your voice has a musical timbre. Do you sing?"

He shivered in mock horror. "Absolutely not. No talent whatsoever, I'm afraid."

"Your creativity lies in another direction, then. Maybe brokering deals." Sweetly serious, she peered at him.

He had trouble swallowing but finally managed to say, "Huh, something to consider."

Ought he to discuss the attraction to her that so often intruded on his thoughts? A jolt of adrenalin knotted his gut, and Shannon's brow puckered. That she easily read him also disconcerted him. It didn't help that, despite Lizzie's words, Ian saw no sign Shannon reciprocated his interest. He pointed out some local landscapes.

Later at the fitness center, Shannon swam in lazy breaststrokes, sidestrokes, and backstrokes. The cool rush of water over her skin lulled her.

"Though a bit short for the role," Ian said, "you remind me of a mermaid."

She smiled. "Name one who's taller."

His rumbling laugh spread gentle ripples toward Shannon. "Since they possess the power to pull sailors to their doom, one assumes a bigger stature."

Shannon laughed at his professorial tone. "Mythical Sea Creatures 101—Sirens sang to lure ships onto the rocks. And I'm not short. You're overly tall."

Grinning foolishly, he raised both hands in defeat.

Just entering the pool and pulling a second man in his wake, a man hailed Ian. When they reached the couple, Ian said, "Shannon, meet Fran and Trevor, trainers."

"Hey." Trevor arced his spread-fingered hand across his thin chest. Fran's weightier head bobbed a quick up and down over Shannon's modest, skirted bathing suit and turned to Ian.

"You live in Vermont?" Trevor asked Shannon.

"No, western Massachusetts." Shannon grinned at him. Had he a tail, Trevor would have whipped the water to a froth.

"I've been rooting for you guys during the pipeline controversies."

Fran jerked a thumb at Trevor. "Any earthy-crunchy cause, and he becomes obsessed. We need to be energy independent—more drilling here, nuclear plants."

Trevor's face reddened. "The disruption to wildlife . . . kill the environment, kill us."

Fran flung out a hand in appeal to the others. "Dramatic much?"

Shannon shook her head. "We haven't yet solved the problem of the safe disposal of nuclear waste or wastewater from fracking. Both require a lot of water. Nuclear plants are placed next to large sources, which makes them vulnerable to floods and hurricanes."

"They'll figure it out," he said. She leaned toward him. Fran felt a pull to also lean in.

Shannon continued, "It's human nature to think, 'Why spend all that money preparing for something that may never happen?' Through much of our industrial history, we've let necessity be the mother of invention."

Fran's eyes took on a triumphant gleam. "Of course."

"That meant after the fact," Shannon said gently. "Problems are dealt with after the damage, not before it could have been stopped and only if the outcry is loud, sustained, and not overshadowed by a new disaster or tragedy."

Shannon focused beyond the men. "The world is so full of unrest. Someone attacks a wind or solar farm, and the local community loses power until it can be repaired. Attack a nuclear plant and cause death and devastation locally that lasts lifetimes. Who knows how far the wind can carry radiation into other countries?"

"Yeah, well, something to think about."

Shannon's eyes drilled into Fran. He could have sworn he heard her say, "Exactly," but her mouth never moved. Shaking himself, he tapped his wrist. "Come on, Trevor. Dinner reservations wait for no man. Nice to meet you, Shannon." It surprised him that he meant it.

Trevor, a puppy dragged from a chew toy, plodded after Fran.

Ian regarded Shannon thoughtfully.

Mischievous eyes glinted back. "Trevor give you grief on the tank you drive?" she asked.

"It requires more fuel," Ian said, "but clean emissions and highway safety outweigh that for me. You stood your ground against the opinionated males."

Shannon grinned at him. "Straightforward, yes or no questions, goal-oriented—typical male perspective. Women think in an it-depends-on-the-circumstances sort of way."

"Chauvinistic, are you?" Ian's eyes crinkled.

"Yes, I hate to admit. One of my worst faults."

A man could learn to live with it, Ian decided. He took her hand to help her out of the pool and kept hold of it as they scurried outside to the hot tub.

"I swear goose bumps have layered over goose bumps," Shannon said. She flinched when her pebbled flesh met steaming water and laughed as Ian flinched. "Pricking needles, right?" She alternately dunked and stood to regulate her temperature.

Ian watched tendrils of vapor twirl about her limbs and frame her face. When they returned to the dressing rooms, his pale skin disturbingly pink, he clutched a towel to his front. He showered in cold water.

Back at the apartment, Lizzie said, "Too freaking cold to go back out. Soup and crackers and the cheese I bought call my name. You two go gallivanting." She nudged Ian. "Build me a fire first, please?"

"Soup sounds fine."

"Aw, sweet. Go. Nowhere fancy, though. She refused to bring dress-up clothes."

"Don't own any. I'm the informal type."

"I'll say—baggy clothes, no makeup."

Shannon lifted a lock of hair.

"Yeah, you went gray really early."

"My grandfather's hair had gone white by the time he turned thirty."

Lizzie's lips pursed. "Your silvers and whites look professionally highlighted, sparkly. You can keep that."

Careful not to land, Shannon batted at her friend's mousse-stiff blond spikes.

A Safe Place

Ian brought Shannon to a candlelit bistro, formerly a mill. The waterwheel revolved outside a window, and a musician plucked at a large harp. The soft ambiance and the back and forth of ideas begun at the pool offset cafeteria-quality fare.

"I worry for my kids," Shannon said, "and future generations. Rivers run out of water before reaching the sea, and the diminishing current impacts their ability to clean out pollutants. Glaciers providing irrigation and drinking water have shrunk or disappeared. Too bad we can't build water pipelines to drought areas from flood plains instead of gas and oil lines. Even our Colorado River ends in Mexico with no water left, something news reporters don't mention much. I wonder how Mexico feels about that. I fear global wars over water rights."

Ian wished to soothe but understood the realities. "As you said to Fran, it's human nature to procrastinate on remedial plans for potential disaster. Global solutions are especially complicated." When it came to battering against inane or corrupt bureaucracies to get supplies to devastated areas, often too late to prevent unnecessary suffering, Ian had more experience than he could share with her.

Listening to Ian, Shannon felt an ease she seldom experienced around men. A vacation relationship had a shelf life, so she felt safe in temporary camaraderie. Her smile warmed.

Ian's body tightened. Shannon's fluidity of mind challenged him, and her passions struck a chord with his own. He was in trouble.

"Tell me about your kids," Ian said. He hadn't thought her smile could glow any brighter.

"Christopher loves playing guitar, writing songs, and video games—the world-building kind. Michael's shy except when it comes to music. He corrects his brother's pitch and has a great ear for harmony. I'm grateful they've always been friends."

24

"I'm an only child," Ian said, "of parents who were only children. Do you have siblings you get along with as well as your sons do?"

Shannon sat back. "I was close to my brother. He died a while ago. My parents and two sisters have . . . different ideas about my choices."

With no inflection to her tone, Ian couldn't read her. He read his instant, absolute need to protect her well enough, though. "They don't support your divorce?"

Shannon laughed. "That was a validating moment for them, the perfect wife and mother failing. There's truth to some old adages. Roger embodies the nice guy who finishes last. He hides his insecurities and inabilities behind the nice guy instead of dealing with them."

Ian saw the mischievous imp he had glimpsed in her earlier peeking out at him.

"I tell them they don't have to like or accept my choices," she said. "They just need to know I'm happy with them."

Unbidden came the thought that he could be happy with her. Instead of anxiety spiking into his belly, exhilaration filled him as his world, his life, seemed to slide onto the path he had been meant to follow.

The restaurant closed, and the couple returned to the resort. Stars shone down on their cottage's dimly lit parking area. Ian swooped around the car's hood to reach Shannon's side. He helped her out with his left hand and pressed her against the door as he closed it.

She looked up uncertainly as his other hand cradled her head. His hooded eyes lowered to her mouth, and he leaned in to kiss her in short sips that afforded no opportunity for protest. Ian lengthened the contact, warming her chilled lips. His large hand roamed, landing to cup her bottom under her bulky winter coat. Her lips parted in surprise rather than invitation, but he took advantage and sinuously inserted his tongue into the heat of her mouth, a heat intensified in contrast to the cold outside air.

Shannon clutched at Ian's coat. The light, sensuous strokes of his tongue had no resemblance to the sex-mimicking tongue-plunging familiar to her. Spikes of unwanted arousal shimmered through her. Ian broke off but continued to pin her body.

Shannon pushed at him. "What are you doing?"

Ian nibbled at her throat as Shannon's pulse built beneath his lips.

"Let go," she said.

"I wasn't the only one participating in that kiss, love."

Her body stilled, her expression indifferent.

Ian suspected nothing good had taught her that control. "The body sometimes overrides the mind if we haven't paid attention to its needs."

"I'd rather listen to my brain, thanks." Shannon resisted the temptation to smack his annoying smirk away and said, "I saw no hint of this."

She was angry and confused but not afraid, Ian noted. "I want you. I think you want me."

"Great. After a few days of casual sex, I go home emptier than I started."

Oh, not likely. Ian knew she hadn't caught what she'd just revealed about her life. His fingers brushed her cheek. He accepted the flinch and let his lips graze her perfectly shaped, freezing ear. She ought to wear a hat.

"No signals. I just figured it out myself, tonight. I'm not proposing an affair." Ian held back a laugh as she rolled her eyes. "It's not a line. I believe God, fate, destiny—whichever you prefer—orchestrated our meeting. I watch you take care of Lizzie and light up when speaking of your boys. I'm offering more than letting you feel like unappreciated china in a hope chest."

Shannon uttered a breathy squeak. "You heard us? Outside, talking?"

"Lizzie's voice carries."

Pink tinged Shannon's blanched cheeks. "Look, Roger may have sucked as a husband, but he's not a bad guy. Complaining about him is just a mean way to let off steam."

Ian studied the resolute little face and realized Shannon had drawn a battle line. Not inclined to forgive a man whose negligence he believed had harmed Shannon, Ian remained undeterred. "I'm surprised no one has tried to lure you before now." Her deepening blush told him the story. "I see someone has or maybe several someones?"

Shannon blinked. A couple of guys had made recent passes, probably some outdated male nonsense about divorced women being easy.

"And your response?"

She refused to answer and didn't know why she had responded to Ian's unsolicited attention.

"Nothing, I bet. They weren't meant for you. Your reaction to me isn't a clue?" Her eyes shuttered, and he drew his own line. "I'm not giving up, Shannon. I will take it slow for the moment." He clasped her arm. "Let's get you inside before you turn into an icicle."

Ian asked for her key card. Rooting in her purse, she fumbled her way to the correct pocket. He inserted the card into the slot.

Inside, Lizzie glanced at Shannon and struggled to stand up. "What's wrong?"

Ian steered Shannon to the fire and removed her coat to give her his body heat and rub her arms for extra warmth. She stood stiffly, refusing to lean into him.

"It's all right. I told Shannon I love her and want to marry her."

Shannon's head snapped around. *That's not what he'd said. Was it?*

Lizzie stood speechless—a first—and short-lived. "Holy shit, I think he means it. Shan?"

Shannon turned to face Ian. "You can't . . . lust isn't love. I don't need a white knight rescuing the damsel . . . " She flicked an impatient hand. " . . . matron in distress from—"

"The life of a nun?" Lizzie glared at Shannon.

"Lust is basic, simple," Ian said, "and worlds apart from my feelings for you. Faith tells me you're mine." He held on to her arms as she tried to step away. "I once held the dream of a family and stupidly let it drop. Not again. I promise to love and cherish you, protect and take care of you."

Lizzie brushed tears away. "I'll let you two work things out." She fled to her room as fast as her arthritis allowed.

Shannon sighed. No help from that quarter. "I'm too old to have more kids."

"Nothing wrong with a ready-made family."

Shannon thought that was his first intentional lie.

Ian ran gentle hands over her shoulders. His eyes teased. "I can't promise this restraint forever, but let's take time to learn about each other." He kissed her good night. "We scheduled meetings through dinner tomorrow. I'll stop by on my way in."

Arms wrapped about herself, Shannon stared into the fire and brooded over her instant response to Ian's kisses. Could it be more than physical? She liked him. Could she trust him? Did she want whatever it was to be more?

❧ ❧ ❧

In the morning, Lizzie decided to pick up presents for her grandchildren. Along the switchback to the resort town, the mountain rose close on the right with pine trees on the left. Lizzie drove and granted Shannon five minutes to brood. "Out with it. What's on your mind?"

"Ever notice marriage vows never mention happiness? The track record of my relationships hardly spells success."

"Relationships? You've had one."

"And this? Swept off my feet by the dashing hero who desires only me? The perfect fantasy, except second marriages have an even higher divorce rate."

"He hasn't pressured you into bed. That says something."

Lizzie parked at a tiny strip mall that managed to look rustic. For a small space, the toy store offered a wide variety. Lizzie loaded her charge card with blue-and-silver-liveried knights and horses, realistic owl and hedgehog hand puppets, and games in fruit-shaped bags. Those brilliant grandchildren would turn up their noses at kitschy souvenirs, so she avoided them.

Shannon held up mugs with CHRISTOPHER and MICHAEL stamped on them. "I'll fill these with fudge."

❧ ❧ ❧

The women drove to the fitness center in the early afternoon. The parking lot had only a few spots left. After changing in the women's locker room, they went their usual separate ways. A man held out a hand to assist Lizzie into the hot tub.

Strafe thought the blond munchkin looked disappointed when he didn't stay to chat, but as usual, she found someone else to jabber to, slinging her tale of woe. She enjoyed the attention. He headed for the pool. Strafe thought her a little old for his taste, but judging from watching them for two days, the other woman sure appealed to Ian. She moved through her exercises like a dancer at the practice barre. Okay, so he wouldn't mind a poke at her.

Strafe entered the water and waited. Something ate at the woman. She repeated several of the exercises and showed no inclination to stop.

28

She had her back turned to him, and he floated into her.

An arm thumped down on his chest. *Shit.*

Eyes wide with concern, the woman whirled around. "I'm so sorry. I didn't see you."

Strafe slowly rubbed his firm chest. "My fault. Was not watching where I was going." He gave her his most charming smile and best fake-Jamaican accent. He'd long ago forgotten his tribal dialect. "I am William."

"Shannon."

The woman smiled, smaller up close, friendly, but without any deeper interest or the unspoken invitation he usually elicited from women. Disappointment at her lack of response surprised Strafe as he briefly touched his lips to her knuckles. "Your arm is not hurt?"

"No, I'm fine."

"I believe I've seen you here before with your husband."

"Our upstairs neighbor sometimes accompanies my friend and me."

Yeah, that hot kiss in front of their cottage was Strafe's kind of neighborly. He edged closer. No harm in adding some pleasure to his fact-finding mission. "Perhaps you would be interested in dinner tonight." Her momentary blink of confusion had him wondering. A woman of her appeal had to be used to come-ons.

"As I said, I'm here with a friend, but thank you. If you'll excuse me."

Strafe blocked her. "Your neighbor, do you know him well?" She leveled an assessing gaze on him. Unable to remember his backstory, he floundered a moment. "I . . . I also conduct business here, perhaps something of interest to him." He shivered as her eyes frosted.

"If you know he's here on business, speak to him directly. He seems approachable."

She glided forward, forcing Strafe to step back. Too many people—he smiled warmly. "Perhaps we will talk again."

He turned his back on the curvaceous ass emerging from the pool. Convinced she had recently met Ian, Strafe doubted he'd gain any pertinent information from her. Still, he wanted more than a polite smile. He'd seen the nothing-held-back version. He'd get another shot at Shannon. Marcus would consider Strafe's belief that Ian seemed hooked on the woman a vulnerability to exploit.

Marcus would be pleased by his report, perhaps enough to give Shannon to him to train. Strafe's breath shuddered through him at that thought. He remained in the cool water until he could walk up the pool steps with his modesty intact.

❧ ❧ ❧

Shannon dismissed the stranger's advances. Plenty of people prowled at resorts. Back at the apartment, Shannon ate peanut butter pie for dinner. Lizzie declined to eat. They spent the evening huddled on the couch, Lizzie clutching a gold cross containing a pinch of her husband's ashes. Though Shannon found it a bit creepy, she was glad it comforted her friend.

"After you married," Lizzie said, "and moved out of town, our friendship got put on hold for a few years. I never told you I left Bobby when he wouldn't quit drinking."

Shannon fit her arms loosely about her friend. "Tell me now."

Lizzie fingered her cross. "Not the best time in my life. I juggled paralegal classes, a job, living at my mother's. The kids' lives barely changed—school, sports, and every other activity under the sun. I doubt the problems between Bobby and me even registered."

Shannon didn't argue. The cross zipped back and forth on its chain.

"Anyway, he did quit, and we were okay."

"Must have been scary before then."

"Yeah, I hate being alone." Lizzie stood up. "Bedtime. Shan, don't choose to be alone if you don't have to. Your kids will be gone sooner than you think."

❧ ❧ ❧

Ian stopped in a few hours later. He kissed Shannon's cheek and searched her shadowed eyes. "Difficult day?"

"Lizzie was upset, and I'm still thrown."

Ian reached out to twine long fingers through her pixyish hair and wondered how to address her insecurities. Surprising him, she stepped closer. He drew her into his body.

"This is good," she said. "Thanks for not getting annoyed. Reassurance is a basic human need, part of feeling safe, I guess."

"Baby, I realize you're conflicted. I'm trying not to push."

30

"If it only affected me, I'd probably be less nervous. Divorce is tough on kids. Preferring another man to their father adds a major crimp."

"I'm here to help you face any repercussions."

Shannon said nothing.

"Mm, used to unfulfilled promises, are you? I'm big on keeping promises." He pressed his lips to her forehead. "I have final trainings and a closing meeting on Sunday. Would you like to join me for a church service of sorts tomorrow? Maybe hike the trails, let nature be our cathedral? We could pick up Lizzie afterward and go to the breakfast buffet at the main lodge."

His breath hitched as a smile illuminated Shannon's lovely face. "That smile intruded on my thoughts all day. I want you."

Shannon tensed, and Ian sighed. "Not meant as a threat, my little puzzle. Reassurance is the key. I'll remember—tomorrow. Something's distracting me tonight."

A slow, thorough kiss left Shannon breathless. Testosterone humming, Ian went upstairs with a grin.

❧ ❧ ❧

Ian called for Shannon in the morning. Clouds obscured the sun. She wore mittens and a hat she'd crocheted in shades from lilac to plum. Ian wondered if the gloom subdued her mood.

Shannon answered the unasked question. "I've always enjoyed gray days, the only time my mother stopped harping at me to stop reading and go outside."

"I have a meeting with the trainers this afternoon, and the training ends tomorrow. I rented the cottage for another week to give us uninterrupted time together."

On the trail, silence grew. "Shannon, talk to me."

"Sorry. My sons are staying with their father. I called them last night and froze, couldn't think of a thing to say. Thankfully, they did most of the talking."

Ian pulled up short. "You ought to have told me, let me help you." He had to laugh at the flustered cluelessness in her eyes and missed the spark of temper flaring to life.

Shannon sidestepped as Ian reached for her. Why would she burden him with her family? Whatever their relationship might become, they hadn't settled one thing yet.

"You think I'm presumptuous." Ian wagged his eyebrows. "Trust me, I've barely begun to presume on you."

Shannon refused to laugh but linked her arm in his, her eyes filled with an impish challenge.

No one shared the tree-lined trail. The lines of Ian's face hardened as his arm beneath Shannon's became unyielding. Her arm jerked away. Ian grasped it firmly and reeled her in inch by inch. He saw uncertainty surface and fade before those sorceress's eyes darkened. Lips twitching, Ian grabbed her hand and continued their walk. Shannon's laughter tinkled on fairy puffs of air.

Ian gave her a scolding look. "We're here to commune with the Almighty."

"I'm grateful," she said, "for this wondrously diverse world and for the people I've met."

Ian lightly squeezed her hand.

They strolled through crunchy brown leaves and past century-old rock walls. Ice-edged streams trickled, some no wider than a hop across. The crisp air smelled faintly of musty leaves, and bare branches afforded breathtaking views of the mountains. Nature's wonder announced itself in every stick and stone.

❦ ❦ ❦

The pair returned for Lizzie. She pranced in front of Ian on the short walk to the lodge. "You two do the deed yet?"

"Elizabeth Victoria."

Lizzie mimicked her friend. "Shannon Rose. That means no. Hang in there, Ian. She's shy. Bet she warms up fine."

Laughter overrode Ian's loyalty and Shannon's aggrieved expression. To make amends, he said, "Shannon Rose, a lovely name."

Ian and Shannon loaded their plates from a buffet of pancakes, strawberry or blueberry compote, and omelets oozing cheese plus ham or bacon. They joined Lizzie, her plate full of iced confections and a spoonful of scrambled eggs, at a table overlooking the valley.

Since Lizzie had allied herself with him, Ian pried into her circumstances.

She sniffled some. "Can you believe Bobby's family thinks I owe them some of his life insurance? They won't believe I didn't even get any.

He said he was covered, but all he had was accidental coverage, which doesn't cover cancer." Indignation fired her appetite. "I opted for the lump sum of his pension. It won't go very far. The VA better not give me grief about survivor's benefits. He had two different cancers at the same time from Agent Orange."

Ian commiserated. "Too many people haven't the resources to prepare ahead of time for drastic financial changes. I have contacts in the VA. If nothing else, I can find out the steps needed to start your claim."

Basking in the male attention, Lizzie had stars in her eyes. The soft glow in Shannon's gave Ian all the thanks he wanted as well as an idea on how to alleviate her concerns.

❧ ❧ ❧

After his late Sunday meetings, Ian stopped in to check on Shannon. She reached on tiptoe to hug him. "What a nice greeting," he said. His cheek scratched hers softly as he angled his head to meet her mouth. Lips and tongues caressed as his hands roamed luscious curves.

Eyes downcast, Shannon pulled back. "I've heard visuals are important to a guy's arousal. I may disappoint you."

Ian's nose nuzzled along hers. "I thought I made it clear I'm attracted to everything about you." He nipped the tip of her nose, a warning not to be foolish that she ignored.

"In clothes. I was fat during my teens and well into adulthood. I learned healthy eating habits for myself and my kids, but you can't undo the damage."

"I love you, baby, however you look. Men are also creatures of action." He let the predatory gleam resurface from the previous day's hike. "Let me love you."

Shannon's muscles clenched from stomach to groin. Sexual response or anxiety—she couldn't tell, which sucked. "Haven't had much success at sex."

"Considering you live like a nun, not surprising."

"Except for the vibrator." She gave him a wicked smile. "I doubt they're recommended gear for nuns."

A muffled laugh snorted through Ian's lips. "You respond to my touch, love."

Shannon conceded the point but left out that her body had never responded to intercourse.

"I have a plan to ease your worries." Ian drew her to the couch and onto his lap. "I've asked a lawyer, an accountant, and my assistant to fly up to meet with us tomorrow night."

"Wow, expensive. I thought your business concerns ended today."

"As they're coming for personal reasons, they'll use my private jet. Your town has an airport for smaller craft. A flight home ought to be easier on Lizzie's back. A hired driver can deliver her van to her door."

Shannon studied the strong-boned face as she put the pieces together. "Not a manager, you own the corporation. Did you grow up wealthy?"

"I've been very privileged."

"You don't strike me as the proverbial spoiled rich kid. Tell me about your family?"

Processed and accepted, as simple as that, he thought. Shannon's curiosity rested on his emotional well-being. Ian doubted that potential ramifications of his wealth to her future crossed her mind.

"My father's grandfather founded the business," he said, "and wanted my father to marry someone whose family would be an asset to the company. My mother's family had a social status they wanted to preserve. Each of my parents divorced their first spouse—no children—and married each other later in life. They called me their extra bonus."

Shannon thought Ian had inherited his parents' streak of Romanticism.

"They died four months apart, both in their eighties. I have no other family."

"Well, that makes your insistence on a relationship more understandable. My Ian, I believe your parents watch over you."

My Ian—the words forged a warm path through his heart. "My parents would have adored you," he said. Remembering his father's protective care of his mother, Ian decided against pressuring Shannon and kissed her good night.

❧ ❧ ❧

The women invited Ian to eat all his meals with them. Neither appeared very chipper at breakfast. He asked them to switch gears and go to the fitness center early. Shannon attempted to cheer up on the drive and arched a playful brow at Lizzie.

"Ian has a surprise. He'll fly us home in his plane and have a driver deliver your van."

Lizzie's jaw dropped. "He owns a whole plane?"

"Half of one doesn't work well."

"Please. He's rich, then."

"Owns the family business. Hasn't mentioned what kind yet."

Both women turned to Ian. "Thanks for including me in the conversation," he said.

Shannon, eyes dancing, stuck her tongue out.

He purred, "Do that again when I'm not driving." To Lizzie, he said, "The corporation is multi-faceted, centered on human services." He could not tell them many branches had been started under the auspices of the Devoted.

In the fitness center, Ian steered the ladies—already wearing their workout clothes—to the exercise machines. Wishing she'd brought a book, Lizzie agreed to ride a bike set on low resistance and trudged along.

Ian demonstrated the proper use of each machine on the circuit for Shannon. He had to adjust the height settings, but the amount of weight her petite frame could handle impressed him. Her muscles pushed and pulled at the machines, exertion dewing her skin. Ian had to shore up his resolve to step back and consider their situation from Shannon's perspective. The call from her family had awakened him to the fact that, though he considered their relationship a done deal, she saw it as leaping off a cliff.

❧ ❧ ❧

Refusing help, Lizzie elected to cook dinner. "Two in this kitchen, they'd be living in sin."

After eating, Shannon loaded the dishwasher for something to do besides brood. Ian hadn't said why he invited his people. She believed the teaching that worry added not a single hour to one's life. Too bad her anxiety turned a deaf ear. She was setting up tea, coffee, and cookies in the living room when the company arrived.

Ian introduced his accountant and lawyer—both in stereotypical, conservative suits, short hair, and glasses—and his assistant Charlotte with office-ready hair and clothes. Even her perfume whispered efficient professional.

Ian sat on the sofa between Shannon and Lizzie. "Remember, love, relieving your concerns is my one goal tonight."

She thought all the mystery counterproductive.

"Ian ordered provisions for your financial security," Harry, the accountant, said and set a prospective account statement on the coffee table. Shannon's arms remained rigidly at her sides.

Lizzie gulped. "Holy shit."

Shannon's voice wavered. "What are you doing, Ian? I won't take it."

"You will." Ian's quiet authority cut through her panic. "Consider it part of a prenuptial agreement. The money affords choices from your heart rather than forced by circumstances." He caressed her troubled face and contrarily smirked. "I could raise the amount to a million."

Shannon's eyes narrowed. The visitors started at the frigid blast. Even Lizzie looked taken aback. Ian laughed and anchored Shannon to the sofa when she tried to get up.

She whapped him squarely in the chest. "Not funny. Are you nuts? Prenups are for after you get married."

The lawyer, Tim, held up a finger. "Actually, prenuptial agreements are always settled before the marriage." A kind smile negated his stodgy pontificating.

Nevertheless, Shannon's face blanched. Ian reflexively released his grip, and she bolted to the mudroom.

"Oh, dear," Charlotte murmured. "Perhaps a bit fast."

Lizzie stood and hesitated. "Ian, a simple life satisfied Shannon. Her family heaped grief on her for throwing away a career for motherhood. Money's a sore spot."

"Thanks. I'll talk to her. Change of plan, people. Wait for my call at the lodge." It did not surprise him to find Shannon's coat gone. Ian threw his on. "Lizzie, any idea where she'd go?"

"The resort has streetlights just at the parking areas. Car keys are still here."

"I'll find her." Ian charged up the stairs and past the reach of the cottage's dim lights. The surrounding trees lumped into blackness. He turned, saw the diminishing back lights of his people's car, and searched in the other direction. Back at the stairs, he shouted her name.

"On the patio." Shannon paced the small yard behind the cottage. Pinhead-sized streetlamps and postage-stamp windows of light winked along the valley floor.

Anger and light seeping through the apartment's window blinds kept Ian upright over the frost-heaved ground. "This is how you solve problems, running away?"

Shannon's scathing glare halted him mid-tirade. Her mild voice contrasted oddly. "Think I could have gotten farther if I meant to run. I certainly wouldn't have answered your bellow." Her arms wrapped around her torso. "This is how you solve problems? Take control and change people's lives without one word to them?"

God, who was she to talk?

"I orchestrated the marriage to Roger, no proposal, made all our major decisions—easier for him. You don't value what you don't work for. Left on his own, I'm not sure he'd have even asked me. Then I dumped him because I was unhappy having to control everything." Shannon willed away the gleam of tears. "I suck at the mating game."

His steps soft and measured, Ian approached. "Your ex isn't a child. He chose, even if by omission. I value you. Baby, I'm asking. Please don't say no to us because you fear failure."

"Please consult me on decisions affecting my future."

Ian lightly clasped her arms. "Outlining expectations is good. Reassurance and consult you—consider it a learning curve." Glad she didn't cry or pull away, he wished she would lean on him. "Shannon, my motive was to provide security, safety. As you said, part of reassurance."

"You can't be my safe place by taking away my choices."

"Never considered myself a safe place for someone. I thought the money would give you security. One-dimensional thinking, I guess."

Shannon shrugged. "It's a materialistic world. Roger and I planned for me to stay home with the kids from the start. I'll never regret it, but my computer skills became outdated, so no important job, stock portfolio, or social prominence—a failure. I care diddly-squat."

Ian pulled her against his chest. "Shush, baby. You are not a failure."

"Didn't say I'm the one who thinks so. Let's go in. Lizzie must be worried."

"I love you. I'll be your safe place. We'll talk, compromise, decide issues together."

Shannon pushed upright. "Put male ego aside and let me be your safe place, too?"

"Deal."

Shannon laid a hand on Ian's heart. "First fight—not so bad."

"Is that what we were doing?" He nuzzled her nose. "You're freezing."

It relieved Lizzie when the couple walked in holding hands. "You okay, Shan?"

"Yeah, just overwhelmed." She dropped beside her friend on the sofa.

"You'll work it out. Better without me. I've overdosed on vacation and touristy stuff. I'm going home, give you guys some privacy."

"You can't handle that drive alone."

"My pilots will bring her home."

Shannon's eye roll pulled him up short. "Right, sorry. Lizzie, would you like a plane ride and your van delivered to you?"

"You're sure? I don't want to be a pest."

Shannon patted Lizzie's leg. "I'm going to make tea." She went to the kitchen.

Ian lowered his voice. "You know full well we need this time together. I won't forget it."

More Than She Seems

Shannon agreed to meet Ian's people the next day after seeing Lizzie off, though she extracted a promise—no pressuring her into anything.

Charlotte helped set up a snack tray. "Ian appears quite off-balance since meeting you."

The weak kitchen lights hampered Shannon's assessment of the woman's intention.

"It's good for him. His life outside of business leaves a bit to be desired." Her eyes twinkled. "I'm not telling tales. Obviously, he loves you. Pardon my familiarity, but I believe you reciprocate his love."

"I'm recently divorced. I'm concerned about starting another relationship so soon."

"Today's meeting is intended to offer options. I hoped to offer friendship and support."

"Thank you." Shannon's chin ducked. "Really."

At the dining room table, Shannon watched for nonverbal communication between Ian and Charlotte and, relieved to see none, judged his assistant sincere. She liked Charlotte.

Harry slid the account prospectus toward Shannon. Unable to pick it up, she read it. "I'm not sure what you expect me to do with this."

"Use it," Ian said, "in any way you deem fit."

"Roger works in a plastics factory, the third shift, now and throughout our marriage. Hates it but shows up every night for the higher shift pay. He's never late with his support payment." She pushed the paper back and forth. "If I agree to this, I'll help him, give him a down payment on a car. His has 180,000 miles."

That stunned Ian into silence. Charlotte nudged him. "Do as you please," he said.

With such a clipped reply, Shannon deemed it better to wait to thank him.

Tim spread more papers on the table. "A possible prenuptial agreement—basic protection for the corporation, a financial settlement should the marriage end."

Elbows on the table, Shannon read it and rubbed her temples. "Seems more than fair but unnecessary until I make a decision." She accepted the personal account to save arguing. She wouldn't use it unless she married Ian.

After his people left, Ian suggested going to the fitness center. He thought it might settle Shannon.

She worked the machines until sweat poured off and her mind quieted. She showered and met Ian at the pool where she watched him slice through the water with the traditional crawl. Having had sufficient exercise, she paddled in place and admired his form while greeting other swimmers.

Attracted by her smile, people stopped to chat. Ian joined them and listened as she coaxed life stories from everyone, making both men and women feel fascinating, an impressive command of the group that left him uneasy. Ian swam to her. "Ready to return to the apartment?"

She nodded and bid everyone good-bye.

❊ ❊ ❊

Assisting Shannon out of her coat, Ian hung it in the entry—one of the numerous old-fashioned courtesies he practiced that she could take or leave, though she appreciated the caring.

"Your choices for dinner," she said, "are steak tips, stuffed tilapia, or leftovers."

Ian snuggled her back to his front. "We can afford to leave the cooking to others. You can even afford to treat." He interpreted her laugh as a positive step toward acceptance.

"I'd rather stay in, if you don't mind."

"Not at all. Fish, please."

Shannon slid a covered dish into the oven. Ian's arms again swooped to gather her into a hug.

"My eagle," she said.

"What?"

"It's a compliment." She rested her cheek on bare skin exposed by his open shirt. The sprinkling of hair tickled her nose. "Predatory eyes,

40

strong nose, bald head, pale skin—but you wear dark clothes. They suit you, handsome fella.”

“No other woman ever called me handsome.”

“Uh-huh. All young and beautiful, I suppose. They weren't meant for you.” Shannon gleefully threw his words back at him.

In retaliation, Ian kissed her senseless until the oven timer interrupted.

At the table, Shannon said, “I'm a homebody. I mean, not a hermit or anything.” Ian covered her fidgeting fingers. “Sorry. Okay, deep breath. Real issue—you want me, but I come with kids. They'll blame you for tearing their life apart and me for choosing you over their father. Neither of us wins any points.”

“Tearing their life apart? Sounds a little drastic.”

“And you, silly man, think you can handle a ready-made family. Teenagers' lives consist of drama.” The light of humor on her face faded. “Divorce and possible displacement from their familiar life come under the drastic column for anyone. I assume you want to stay in Boston. We've always lived in a small town.”

“You told me a relationship is a two-way street. Doesn't that mean voicing what you need, such as telling me you'd rather stay where you are?”

“Never really had to since I made the decisions. Guess that learning curve will be for both of us.” Shannon's brow knit. “I grew up in central New Jersey, not yet New York's suburb but getting there. When I was six, we came up to western Massachusetts to visit my grandparents. It felt like home the moment I saw it. I moved there right after college.”

“We'll need to live in Boston until we find property in your town.”

Shannon searched his eyes. “You're sure? Wouldn't you miss Boston?”

Wouldn't instead of won't—the difference was not lost on Ian, nor the implied indecision. “Boston is a short plane trip away and not all that far by car.” He rubbed the back of his head. “Being accepted by your sons concerns me more.”

“Yeah, you don't know my kids, let alone love them. Makes dealing with them harder.”

“I disagree. Looking at them, I'll see you, remember what's best for you. Besides, I'd play a supportive role for your discipline rather than an authoritative role.”

His earnest expression unknotted knots Shannon hadn't realized she harbored. "The take-charge guy's okay at being relegated to the sideline?"

"It's training." *Damn.* Her brows lifted in curiosity. "I have friends in all kinds of family scenarios. My turn to clear the table."

Ian mentally shook himself. Before taking over his corporation, he had been a Protector of Jasirey, one who vowed to protect and serve her and who must follow wherever she led. Every one of the Devoted knew the Protector's top tenet. In raising her children, Jasirey ruled. Unable to deny the signs any longer, Ian breathed around the lump clogging his throat. Ironic if, after leaving the Protectors, the one woman he was blessed to love turned out to be Jasirey.

Could I share Shannon with the Devoted? On the other hand, Ian still hoped to be a father. Devoted lore foretold many children for Jasirey, multiracial children. Shannon would be forced to choose other fathers as well. Obligated to contact the island for guidance, he promised himself to do so as soon as they got home.

Ian ran gentle fingers over Shannon's cheek. "May I stay here now? Everything still at your pace."

She drew a steadying breath. "Such a sweet man."

"Mm. Patient, anyway."

Shannon tiptoed to press her cheek to his. "I promise not to tell anyone."

"Not usually into spanking, I may change my mind in your case."

"Big, tough guy."

"Your guy." Ian saw the carotid artery visibly pulsing in her neck and rubbed her back. "I'll run upstairs to grab a few things. Lizzie gave me her key card. I'll meet you in the bedroom."

Swift action—why prolong her anxiety?

❧ ❧ ❧

Shannon owned no clothes one could consider remotely sexy. She rarely shaved in the winter. Who was there to see? She realized that putting off shaving put off the decision to have sex. Yet there she sat, her stomach hurting. She did a series of calming breathing techniques. Calmer, she opened her eyes and inhaled sharply. Ian watched from the doorway.

He gathered her close. "Nice and slow, baby." He laid her face-down on the bed, placed a bottle beside her, and disturbed by her mute tension, straddled her legs to stroke over her clothing from neck to buttocks. He took his time peeling off layers, first to softer underwear and finally reaching warm skin.

Ian felt fit muscle on Shannon's thighs and ass. He enjoyed skimming his hands over her curvaceous shape. Kissing her cute nose, they locked gazes as he rolled Shannon to her back. An urge to punch the ex-husband bloomed red as he watched her struggle not to cover her nakedness. He buried his face in her neck and breathed in her scent to shake off the urge.

"I love you." He filled his hands with her heavy breasts, palms brushing the hardening tips, tiny for such full orbs. His hands stroked from collar bones to a pouching tummy he didn't mind in the least. Ian pulled off his shirt and slid his firm torso along her softness.

Shannon ran her hands over Ian's back and became fascinated by the novel sensation of individual muscles. When his teeth raked down to her breasts, her mind blurred. He nibbled and sucked back and forth, increasing the pressure until a pulsing wave rushed from tingling breasts down Shannon's arched spine and crested in hot wetness.

Ian nuzzled the sweet curve between her neck and shoulder while she caught her breath.

"Dear God," she said on a gust of air.

"Thank you for the promotion, love, but it's Ian, just plain Ian."

"Smart ass."

"Very, and it provides excellent locomotion to an even cleverer penis." He kissed her between giggles. "Make fun. See if I do anything else for you." Her impish glint sent his pulse racing. "Undress me," he murmured huskily.

Shannon refused to let nerves hamper her, though her hands fumbled a bit unclasping his belt buckle and unzipping the fly. Roger had fit in her hand. Ian might take two, two and a half. Granted, she had small hands.

Ian smothered a laugh as Shannon sat blinking, a little bewildered. "Trust me to take care of you. Patience—" He tapped the nearby bottle. "—and lots of lubricant. Your body will adjust and feel really good about it." Her smile made him feel better than good.

Shannon watched Ian kick off his pants and boxer briefs. In a teasing tone, she said, "Do condoms fit you?" His expression went blank as hers became disappointed. "You don't have any."

"I didn't expect to meet the love of my life this trip."

"Yet you packed lubricant." Amusement tinged her rueful familiarity with the necessity for self-gratification.

"I've been celibate a while. No STDs. I'm sure you can say the same."

"It's not just diseases. No good eggs left, but pregnancy is still an issue—or miscarriage."

Ian leaned back. "Where are you in your cycle?"

"I've never been regular but probably past ovulation."

Her soft fingertips soothed Ian's furrowed brow. "I'm sorry I can't give you a family," Shannon said. "A younger, fertile woman—"

"I'm disappointed you would put me aside so easily."

"You deserve to be happy."

The simple sincerity undid Ian. "Marry me, be my family. We'll both be happy." He kissed her nose. "That wasn't the formal proposal." Ian slanted his lips over Shannon's, nudging hers to part. Slow and deep, the long kisses seeped into both body and heart. "I want you, my love. You willing to take the chance?"

Shannon's eyes widened, but she nodded. He flipped her, ass in the air, spread the labia, and granted free rein to his flexible tongue. He inserted a finger. So wet—and tight. He slid in another finger, in, out, and around, stretching, inhaling her delectable scent, tasting. Her rich saltiness fired his blood. Ian throttled back to liberally lubricate himself and her.

"Ian. Roger and I didn't fit this way."

"Fit? Oh." She'd never had sex from behind. Hearing her embarrassment, Ian collected himself. He had intended to take her face to face but stayed where he was. "Trust me, baby. Let me handle everything this first time."

"I want it to be good for you, too."

"Believe me, that's seldom a problem for men."

Shannon started to laugh, but Ian's single deep thrust pushed the air from her lungs. The ready-to-burst fullness felt alien and not particularly enjoyable.

"Shannon, relax. You'll snap me in two here." Ian caressed the lovely, cushioned ass until, one by one, her muscles let go. He gently rotated his hips to help her body adjust, then moved in slow, shallow strokes until she moved in instinctive counterpoint. Able to feel that she needed more stimulation, Ian reached around to alternately rub, flick, and pull on her clitoris.

Unfamiliar spikes of pleasure had Shannon emitting noises she'd never heard from herself. Self-conscious, she struggled to move as she thought Ian needed her to.

"Easy, baby, don't fight it." Ian's large hands kneaded, soothed, and grasped her hips. He surged deeper, faster, and steadily built up a wave of pure sensation.

Shannon anchored her hands in the sheets and crested in a glorious, whooshing release. She dimly felt Ian shuddering behind her. He guided her to collapse on their sides, still joined. After their breathing softened, he cupped her vulva and slowly withdrew. Another orgasm set off sparks behind Shannon's eyelids and left her spent body quivering.

Ian meant to get up for a washcloth, but holding Shannon's warm, pliant body, he heard her breathing even out into sleep, and he followed.

❧ ❧ ❧

In the morning, Ian's body longed for a replay of the night before. Assuming it would be too much for Shannon's body, unused to regular sex, he settled for caresses. Her teeth nipped at his throat and shoulder as her tongue soothed the slight sting. "Uh, baby, we ought to shower."

"Uh-huh." Shannon slipped the sheet past the tent at Ian's groin. His indrawn breath assured her of the effectiveness of the move. His flat, toned stomach invited kisses. She hoped it wasn't petty to be grateful that, despite his obvious fitness, some skin sagged. She rested her cheek on his abdomen and tracked a finger up and down his engorged flesh. No sagging there.

Ian stroked her hair and tacitly encouraged. He contemplated removing the sheet she'd wrapped about her body but, curious concerning her knowledge and reluctant to interrupt the playfulness, refrained.

Shannon picked up the lubricant, warmed the odorless liquid between her palms, and applied it in broad strokes with one rotating hand. The other massaged his perineum. She peered at Ian and blushed. "The sex-technique video I learned this from said guys sometimes enjoy having their anuses massaged."

Ian forced strangled words past his throat. "Sex video?"

"No laughing, you. You're my guinea pig and at my mercy."

"Then please have your way with me. Never mind the anus." He held her small hand up to his. "You'll need a sex toy for prostate massage."

Shannon buried her face in his stomach. "The video didn't show that."

Ian gulped air as she grasped the base of his shaft and bathed the head with a swirling tongue. Her hand stroked while she alternately licked or sucked. Ian's hands threaded through her hair. His hips bucked as he drove deeper into her mouth. Her grip on him assured not too far. Shannon's hand and mouth tightened and, helpless under the onslaught, Ian came. She let his semen dribble and used a tissue to clean him.

A smile playing on her beautiful mouth, she laid her head on Ian's shoulder. He traced her succulent lower lip. "Happy with yourself?"

"And you." Her gaze remained on his chest. "Do you mind I didn't—? I wasn't ready?"

His curled finger raised her flushed face. "Your comfort is my first priority, and bluntly, my pleasure had nothing to do with the handling of my ejaculate." He patted her ass. "Great technique for someone needing a training video for blow jobs."

"Gross."

Ian grinned at the teenage spin on the word. "Let's shower together and see what I can do for you." She squirmed, and he cocked an eyebrow. "I've already explored and enjoyed every lovely inch of you."

"It's different in bed."

When Ian's brow raised another notch, Shannon drilled a finger into his ribs. "Admit it. Standing, gravity's harder to ignore."

"Love, why this negative body image? Did your ex say you displeased him?"

Shannon sat up. "You can't blame all my marital problems on Roger. I was naïve, thinking marriage and parenthood would make him grow up." She sighed. "Once, clothes held in front, I dredged up the courage to walk naked from the shower to our bedroom. He suggested I go to Weight Watchers. In fairness, that was before I lost weight."

Ian jumped out of bed, plucked Shannon from the sheet, and slowly twirled her around in front of him. Hectic red stained her cheeks, and he knelt to tongue circles across her belly. "Delicious—soft—wiggly."

Without hair to muffle the sound, the slap Shannon landed on the top of his head made a satisfying smack. Laying a hand on her bottom, Ian accepted her teasing challenge with one of his own.

She burrowed into him. "Lizzie bragged about multiple orgasms, talked about their connection," she told him. "I thought she exaggerated."

Ian cradled her face and saw a bewildered, painful mix of emotions in her eyes.

"Never had much response from penetration," she said, "by either man or machine. Kind of thought my body didn't work right."

Her eyes filled with gratitude. "Thank you."

❦ ❦ ❦

The rest of the morning went downhill. Shannon's kids expected her to phone them again that night. Ian took her for a long walk on the trails to combat the adrenaline spiking with her worries of how her sons would react to him asking her to marry him, but when they returned to the apartment, she continued to pace.

When she said no to a trip to the bakery for a sticky bun, Ian said, "Why don't we take the boys to my home in Boston for the rest of our vacation? Give them a chance to get to know me. The plane can be here this afternoon."

Shannon readily agreed and called her sons about her early return but didn't mention Ian and barely spoke to him while packing. Ian's mood soured as he watched her pick at lunch. He also had little to say. Shannon cleaned the dishes and brought her packed suitcase out to the mudroom.

"Leave that to me," he snapped.

She straightened abruptly. "Ian, my kids are still mourning the death of my marriage and blaming me, my failure to make it work. You can't put a timetable on grief."

Ian jumped up to press penitent kisses over her face. "I'm sorry, love." He smiled slightly. "You'll have to forgive me, though, if I believe it was more his failure."

"I love you, my Ian."

For Ian, the sun rose.

❦ ❦ ❦

Ian had a rental car waiting when they landed at the small airport in Shannon's town where they would pick up her kids. Though the

47

town boasted an airport, it had no cab service. Shannon directed him
to a nineteenth-century farmhouse rehabbed into four apartments, two
to a floor. Paint peeled from the clapboards, and pigeons roosted on
the waste-stained roof. The upstairs hall reeked of garbage. Unlocking
several locks, Shannon led Ian into a living room barely large enough to
hold a couch, a bookcase, a nineteen-inch TV, and a table with a desktop
computer. He gratefully drew in a deep breath of unsullied air.

Shannon hung up his coat on a hall tree, no closet. "I'm waiting for a
raise to look for something better," she said.

"Not necessary."

Her wary eyes flew up to his.

"Stay with me in Boston while we look for a house here. Homeschool
the boys in the interim."

"No," Shannon said. "I'm not ready. I have a job."

"A job you no longer need."

"And here," Shannon said, "the privileged upbringing shows
through. Roger pays for the kids' insurance, but I get mine through
work. Paying for a policy outside of work's group rate would plow a wide
swath through the account."

Shannon kissed his cheek and gestured to the claustrophobic kitchen.
"There's tea in the cabinet by the fridge. The water's good out of the
tap. There's leftover food in the cooler if you're hungry. I'll be back in an
hour or so. She gave him a teasing smile. Hope my car starts after sitting
so long."

Ian admired Shannon's skill at sidestepping arguments and accepted
that he would not win any regarding finances. He had agreed to stay
in her apartment while she fetched her kids and prepared them for his
presence. He explored while he waited.

❧ ❧ ❧

Large-boned and pudgy, Roger pecked Shannon's temple and feigned
an apology for the unkempt house. He had kept the family home since the
mortgage amounted to little more than rent for an apartment. With no
DIY skills, Shannon knew she hadn't the money to hire others for upkeep.
Thankfully, her landlord kept the apartment building up to code.

Christopher, fifteen, and Michael, thirteen, had several inches on
their mother and bent down to return her hug.

48

"How's Lizzie?" Roger asked.

"As well as you'd expect. Boys, go get your things. Give your dad and me a minute."

Shannon gestured at Roger to sit. She tried not to wince at the food-stained armchair. "They won't be long, so I'll get right to the point. I met someone at the resort. It might be serious."

Roger deflated as she crushed his hope for a reconciliation. "What about my sons?" His body stiffened. "Nobody, by God, is taking my sons away from me."

"Of course not. He's willing to relocate here. He lives in Boston. I'm taking the kids to his house for the rest of their school vacation to get to know him."

Roger seesawed between anger and panic. She still handled the bills and knew he was hopeless with money.

"We'll work it out," she said softly.

"If they'll do it with you, they'll do it to you. I never cheated."

Shannon paused for several moments and managed not to throttle him. "I waited, hoped for years, endured—not being wanted, frustrated to the point of literal physical pain. And just for the record, you— We're not married anymore."

Shannon inhaled slowly, exhaled, and really looked at Roger. He had gained weight, his hair had grown grayer, and his mustache drooped over his upper lip. Romantic love between them had died, but as the father of her children, he would always be family. Praying she was making the right choice, Shannon leaped.

I'm not waiting any longer, she thought. She squatted in front of Roger's chair to gaze eye-to-eye and waited until her calm demeanor soothed and lulled him.

"You will buy a membership at our town's workout center," she said, her voice nonconfrontational, "and join the healthy eating support group at the hospital. You will do this for yourself and to make sure you'll be around for your sons." She patted his knee. "Okay?"

Roger blinked and slowly readjusted to reality, a familiar sensation from all the times his wife had helped him to cope and probably the one thing he missed the most since she'd moved out.

"Okay," he said.

Shannon considered her ability to sway people neither a beneficial nor a unique gift, and despite believing that such manipulation of a person bordered the line between helping and dictating, she had over the years let her reservations blur and without conscious thought used her gift to create harmony between Roger and herself until harmony alone no longer sustained the marriage.

Back in the car, she hoped for a minute to settle, but Michael said, "How come Dad looked so weird when we left?"

Deep breath, Shannon reminded herself. "I met someone in Vermont. His name is Ian. He's asked me to marry him. We're going to visit his house in Boston for the rest of our vacation so you three can get to know one another." She did her best to soothe her stunned sons and answer their questions.

On the plane, Ian kept up the conversation and learned that Shannon and her sons had visited Boston only on school trips to the science museum. "Well," he said, "we'll have plenty of things to explore. The Freedom Trail includes the Old South Meeting House where the Boston Tea Party was planned and the Old North Church. Perhaps you're familiar with the account described in the poem 'Paul Revere's Ride' by Henry Wadsworth Longfellow of the potential British attack signaled by 'One if by land, two if by sea.' Well, those lanterns were displayed at the top of the steeple of the Old North Church. By the waterfront, Faneuil Hall has a marketplace and art exhibits."

Christopher looked up from his lap. "Is there enough room for us at your place?"

"I own a large Victorian house with plenty of rooms and lots of frou-frou decorations your mother will like."

Shannon smiled. "And this nice big house no doubt has a nice big kitchen where you'll expect me to go around barefoot in a frilly, frou-frou apron."

Ian blinked, heard the boys' snickers, and grabbed the bull—or woman—by the horns. "Feel free to run around in any state of undress you please. It will certainly please me." He planted a kiss over her rising snarl. "I have a house manager, Everett—his last name, but he prefers it. A British thing, I think."

Impressed by Ian's courage, Michael asked, "Is Everett a butler?" *That might be cool.*

"Not exactly. I rely on him as a friend and to run our home. He lives there, though he has his own living area."

Michael's shoulders drooped as he looked at his mom. "How come you and Dad couldn't work things out? You know, tell him what to do."

Shannon finger-combed Michael's dark blond mushroom cut. Christopher avoided Ian's gaze. "You can't control other adults' choices," Shannon told them. "We talked about the things your father and I tried to make a better marriage—books, classes, counseling. Nothing worked for long."

"Maybe it wasn't his fault," Christopher said. "Dad forgets easy."

Shannon gently pulled Michael's fingernails away from his teeth. "I wondered the same thing, stayed, and grew angrier and more frustrated. It became harder just to be nice to your father. I decided I have the right to a better life, to be happy. I am sorry for dragging you both along when you had no say, but I believe things will get better in time—for your father, too."

Ian could see Shannon's tension. Deciding she and the boys could use a break, he handed the teens over to the co-pilot for a visit to the cockpit and pulled Shannon onto his lap. "I studied the family photos on the bookcase while you went to get the kids."

A younger Shannon, her shoulder-length hair wavy and auburn, had beamed at an infant Christopher whose dark tufts of hair had changed to tight curls the same color his mother had back then. In another, each with midnight blue eyes alight, the boys climbed a slide. Older, they smiled for middle-school graduation pictures.

Exploring the apartment had taken just fifteen minutes, and Ian had seen no antiques—no more than a box or two of keepsakes. He could have stowed everything on the plane.

"You were right, love. I was unprepared for their depth of grief, but your love radiates from every pore, something for Christopher and Michael to rely on as you can rely on me. I won't press about an immediate decision, but in the next few days, we should discuss giving notice to your job and moving to Boston for the short-term."

"I love you, my Ian. I parked in the driveway of the apartment, took one look at the place, and told the kids we're getting married. I think talking to Roger cleared up a lot for me. I trust you and want a life with you."

Ian gathered Shannon against him. "I can't think of anything intelligent to say. Except, thank you. Thank you, baby."

She squeezed tight. "Be prepared for pushback from the kids," she sighed. "Probably from me, too, when fear takes hold."

Ian's hands framed her face, his mouth settling reverently over hers.

❧ ❧ ❧

Ian lived in a neighborhood of half a dozen Victorian homes on spacious, landscaped properties with tree-lined drives.

Everett welcomed them at the door. A man of average height in his late sixties, he wore slacks and a sweater. Shannon smiled at Michael's disappointment. Everett led them into a living room where he had arranged coffee, tea, cocoa, sandwich triangles, apples, and homemade sugar cookies on a serving cart before a crackling fireplace.

Ian introduced Shannon as his fiancée. She beamed at him and instinctively dimmed her smile, he noted, before turning to Everett.

The older man bowed, something he rarely did. "I had begun to despair of Ian finding someone to love. My dear, you are a welcome addition to our home." Shannon's smile transformed to a high-watt glow. Everett stood transfixed. She reached up and kissed him on the cheek. He did some beaming of his own before clearing his throat. "Please sit. Be comfortable."

The boys grabbed several cookies apiece and dunked them in mugs of cocoa. If Everett disapproved, he didn't let on. Not one for formal manners, Shannon merely reminded her sons to use coasters and napkins. Everett left them on their own. The teens tried the sandwiches, ate four, and ended with apples.

"I remember those days," Ian said under his breath.

"Jealous?"

"Being older has its compensations." His long fingers played along her neck and back.

The boys stared, glanced at each other, and drank their cocoa.

After their snack, everyone returned to the foyer to climb the wide staircase leading upstairs. Tongue-tied after learning that they each got a room of their own, Michael and Christopher goggled at the large bedrooms and queen beds.

"Your laptops and smart phones will be here tomorrow," Ian said.

Shannon rounded on him.

"Oops," he exclaimed. "Did I overstep?"

"Yes. I expect you to talk to me first about any decisions involving my kids."

Ian pulled her to his side. "I noticed homework papers and bills by the desktop computer. I assumed you all share it." He kissed her hair. "I have one of each for you, too. Everett got a discount for the package deal."

At the twinkle in his eyes and the excitement in her sons', Shannon knew she was sunk.

"She has a track phone," Christopher said, "just for car emergencies."

Ian glanced at Shannon. "So, rules on texting and internet use?"

"Such as? I've never texted. We mainly use the internet for research."

Christopher squirmed in sympathy and said to Ian, "Means you should have thought about that before."

Ian winked at the teens. "I got the gist." He laughed as Shannon continued to look at him expectantly. "Baby, we need to update your social-media skills."

She made a face. "Don't have much use for it."

"Well, I guarantee your sons will. It won't hurt to learn your way around."

"I check their Facebook pages. The negativity and bullying floor me. And I'm talking about from the adults. 'Let's see who shares this picture to support'—whatever. 'Only one percent care enough. I'm part of the one percent'—hinting something's wrong with you if you don't share it. Self-righteous, armchair crap. Wonder if they ever leave those armchairs to actually do something besides touch a keypad. Pisses me off."

"Apparently." The boys grinned, and Ian said to them, "Give me time to bring your mom into the twenty-first century. We'll get back to you on the rules."

"Okay," Christopher said, "and thanks, Ian."

"Yeah, thanks," Michael said.

Heads together, the brothers stayed to explore their rooms. Their father didn't talk back to their mom—not that Ian had either, exactly. She seemed not to mind anyway, and he touched and kissed her more in one day than their father ever had. And calling her baby? It gave them a weird, hollow feeling.

Ian showed Shannon the master bedroom. A king-sized bed dwarfed the other furniture.

"That's not Victorian," she said.

"No, my feet hung over." Ian grinned at Shannon's laugh and directed her toward a delicately carved nightstand. Daffodils filled the vase she'd admired in Vermont. "Welcome home."

Possibilities

Shannon asked why Everett didn't join them at dinner.

"He's tradition-bound," Ian said. "Eats in the kitchen even when I'm alone."

At least the man set the dishes on the table and let the group serve themselves.

After dinner, Ian said, "I have a few things to attend to in my office. Make yourselves at home."

The boys had brought a game system. Assured they knew how to hook it up, he showed them the TV room. Shannon forbade TVs in their rooms.

Ian entered his office, centered himself with a few deep breaths, and connected to island security, who transferred him to Master Kai.

The elderly master greeted him. "Ian, how pleasant to hear from you."

"I'm calling to share good news." Ian's grin burst. "I've found my wife."

"My sincerest congratulations."

The glow in Ian's eyes dimmed, and the older man waited for him to ease into what else prompted the call.

"Shannon fills spaces———" Ian's hand skimmed his head. "Her smile, when she aims it at me, I feel," he paused, "the world expands—"

"She embodies possibility for you."

Ian gave a slight bow. "I believe I've found our lady."

"So I gather. She is there with you?"

Ian nodded.

"Introduce us, please."

Ian found Shannon lost in daydreams and staring into the living-room fireplace. Sensing his presence, she smiled and warmed his heart, though it thumped in both pain and pleasure. "Sorry to disturb your reverie, love. A friend wishes to meet you online. Come along?" Setting her hand in his, Shannon followed him to the office where an Asian man regarded her pleasantly from a laptop.

"Hello, Shannon. Congratulations. Ian has told me of your engagement."

A loud shout startled her as three men burst into the room. Knowing how difficult bringing Shannon to the attention of the Devoted was for Ian, Master Kai had called in Lee, Liu, and Fael.

Ian's face lit. "Gentlemen, come meet my fiancée."

"Seriously?" The voice boomed from a massive man sporting dreadlocks.

Goodwill shining from them, the men appraised her. Ian stood behind Shannon, his hands covering her shoulders. "Shannon, the mountainous individual is Lee, the medium-sized one Liu, and Fael."

Lee smiled broadly. "How did a beast like you entice such a sweet beauty?"

"Believe it or not, these three are the closest I have to friends."

Liu's dark eyes glinted. "Have Ian bring you to visit. Perhaps you will prefer one of us."

Shannon's laughter bubbled and filled Ian's friends with joy for his good fortune. But Ian tensed, and she twisted to check on him. The men looked worriedly at him and quizzically at her. She crossed her arms to lay her hands over his and seemed fragile in comparison until one observed the fiercely protective stance.

Master Kai gave Ian's team a warning look. "You must visit us, Shannon. Soon, Ian, yes?"

"Within the next week."

Annoyance crossed Shannon's face.

"Shannon," the older man said, "knowing Ian, I imagine he wishes to officially present you to his friends—family really. We live on an island, a lovely place for a few days away."

"I've just been on vacation and have to return to work."

"We could go this weekend," Ian said. Shannon's eyes sparked and not in the way he liked.

"Do not be upset," Fael said, his gold eyes focused intently on her, intending to soothe. She shut him out, a percussive door slam he felt physically and mentally. The woman had power.

Master Kai said, "Ian, share a few facts to tempt your fiancée to visit. I am truly pleased for your good fortune and hope to meet you in person, Shannon."

As soon as the screen darkened, Shannon whirled on Ian.

"Is that your strict mom face?"

"You're not a child." She eyed him and breathed, "Distraction won't work."

Ian caressed her stiff body. He couldn't blame her, but what to say to convince her to go? "I ought to explain what I do outside of business."

"Who was the older man? You didn't introduce him."

"Master Kai."

"As in a martial-arts sensei?"

"Similar," he said. "He trained me. I trained Liu, Fael, and Lee and commanded them on covert missions."

"For the CIA or something?"

He smiled at her wide-eyed wonder. "Something. I'm not free to share details." Close to the truth. "Nothing as glamorous as James Bond."

Shannon blushed. "Why the rush to visit? You said an island?"

"Small place, off the radar. It's beautiful. I'd like you to see it."

She twined her arms around his neck and regarded him coolly. "You aren't telling me everything. You still lead these missions?"

"Too grueling for a man my age." Nearly true. "I can better explain on the island."

"The one called Lee reminds me of those huge brown bears. Bet he came in handy."

Ian buried his face in her hair.

"You miss it a lot?"

"I'd rather spend the rest of my life with you." Completely true.

❧ ❧ ❧

Breakfast in the bedroom had always been Ian's morning routine. Everett assumed that Ian had had the good sense to inform his fiancée. Judging from her startled yelp, however, he had not.

Ian swung his legs from under the bedclothes, Shannon clutching at the sheet. He managed to squelch his laugh. "Sorry, love. Everett is used to me waking up naked."

"Well, I'll make sure I wake up clothed."

Everett's lips twitched. He set the tray down and retreated.

Eyes gleaming, Ian leaned in to kiss her. "Good morning, baby."

Later in the shower, cramps announced Shannon's period. She agreed to a quiet day in the library while Ian took the boys to the Boston Aquarium where they spent most of their time at the shark tank. Ian had to smile when he offered to buy a keepsake for the teens in the gift shop. They shot furtive glances at him as they tried to figure out the protocol of a situation entirely outside their realm of experience.

"I'm sure your mom won't mind a trinket or T-shirt." Ian's eyes crinkled. "It's not like we're talking about a computer."

The boys grinned, their smiles near copies of their mother's. Michael picked a toy baby seal, its white fuzzy fur and dark eyes quite lifelike, and Christopher, a sparkly geode. He looked shyly at Ian. "Could we get a piece of amethyst for Mom? She likes purple."

A shift in Ian's heart told him a wall had been breached. At lunch, he was impressed when the teens added a salad to the staple of cheeseburgers and fries. "Your mom said she told you we plan to get married."

Michael swallowed a large chunk of bun practically whole. "And we have to live here."

"Temporarily. We're looking for a house in your town."

"What about our friends until then?" Michael's hand inched toward his mouth.

Well, shit. Risk Shannon's ire or leave the boys hanging? "Uh, you spend time with your dad every week so you can see your friends then. And you can call or Skype them from here."

Christopher glanced at his brother. "Do we have to, like, follow your rules?"

Ian smiled, more secure here. "I'll follow your mom's rules."

"But it's your house."

"Our house. Your mom knows a lot more about parenting than I do."

"Okay." Christopher shrugged. "Like Mom says, she deserves to be happy."

Michael nodded and lifted a fry to his mouth.

After dinner, Ian gathered everyone in the living room and gave Shannon the chunk of clear amethyst quartz they'd bought for her. She kissed him and the boys for thinking of her.

"I also wanted to discuss what everyone wants in our new house," he said. "Everett gave me his wishes for his room, the kitchen, and the laundry room."

"Whoa," Shannon said, "I know Everett's used to running your house, but—"

"Talk to him. I'm sure you can work everything out to your mutual satisfaction."

Shannon fumed at Ian's blasé attitude, but inherent honesty made her acknowledge that uncertainty—okay, fear—fueled her adrenaline spike. Ian didn't need her to keep house, do yard work, or juggle finances. Scary prospect. She might need to reinvent herself for this marriage.

Ian spread papers on the coffee table to represent rooms. He started with the boys whom he knew itched to return to video games on the new-to-them smart TV. "I thought, as well as a bathroom between your rooms, you might like a common room for schoolwork and friends you entertain together."

"Sweet." Christopher high-fived his brother.

For the bathroom, they wanted a walk-in shower. Neither enjoyed sitting in a tub, a quirk shared with their mother. Ian suggested a bidet, which they gave enthusiastic approval to once he explained its purpose.

"It's hard to keep clean," Michael said, "with a bunch of hair back there."

Ian swallowed hard, damned if he'd embarrass the boy and pleased Michael was comfortable telling him such personal details. He frowned at Shannon's luminous smile and patted her ass, a warning to stop distracting him. He sketched the work and entertainment sections of the common room and suggested a snack area, including a mini fridge and microwave.

"You guys return all dirty dishes to the kitchen," Shannon said. "Any mold gardens, and you lose the privilege." She ignored Michael's eye roll and, except for vetoing fireplaces in their rooms, left the planning to them.

Christopher suggested recycling bins. Sorting paper, plastic, and metal had entertained the boys as toddlers and become habit. They learned that common items like water bottles and plastic bags winding up in the ocean contaminated or injured fish, birds, and turtles. They didn't balk at reusable water bottles.

Prepackaged junk food was harder to give up. Palm oil plantations produced the oil used in everything from dessert foods to salad dressings. They also destroyed endangered animals' habitats and worsened climate change by tearing out carbon-absorbing, oxygen-producing trees.

The boys also knew that rampant consumerism—constantly upgrading to the newest game system, phone, or TV—left discarded electronics that often got shipped to poorer countries where unprotected people, even children, melted off the toxic coatings on precious metals to sell them.

Human and economic growth versus good planet stewardship were difficult concepts to teach. A tight budget had probably been a blessing for reining in her sons' commercial appetites. Considering their soon-to-be new circumstances, Shannon would have to rethink her strategy.

Both kids wanted bunk beds to accommodate friends staying the night. Christopher asked for extra outlets to plug in guitars and amplifiers.

"Ah, in that case," Ian said, "we ought to soundproof your room."

Shannon raised an eyebrow. "That's not permission to play at ear-shattering levels."

"The music sounds stupid if it isn't loud."

"Sorry, it's my job to keep you whole, including your hearing, till you're grown."

Since his mom never backed down on health stuff, Christopher shrugged in resignation.

"Any preference on house styles?" Ian asked the boys.

"Castles are cool," Michael said. Christopher gave a thumbs up.

Shannon laughed. "You're excused, you nuts." Grinning, the boys returned to the TV room and their video games.

"Watching you parent," Ian said, "I see that you're a bossy little thing. It's strangely arousing."

She stuck her tongue out. He attempted to capture it, but she evaded. "Plans, mister."

"Spoilsport." Ian switched papers. "For us, I suggest a bedroom with a sitting area and dining nook for times we want to be lazy and sleep in."

Shannon poked him. "Wonder if I'll get any rest on these lazy days." She pretended to ignore his sexy smirk. "I'd like storage space for my craft supplies."

Ian nestled her against him and leaned his cheek against hers. "Close your eyes."

She shifted to peer at him. "What are you up to?" He raised an eyebrow. "Good dad look, by the way," she observed. Pressed back against him, Shannon closed her eyes to please him.

"Describe your dream house."

"Solar energy's good."

"Mm hmm, and for you alone, what?"

"Flower gardens planned to bloom all season would be nice, though I prefer growing vegetables. I'd love a greenhouse to start them early and to grow some things yearlong."

"What style house?"

"Don't know much about styles. Funny, Michael mentioning a castle. My grandparents' house had bay windows stacked on each floor that looked like turrets. I loved them as a child."

"Your biggest fantasy for a house?"

"In my last home, I had two feet of countertop workspace. I dreamed of enough room for a food processor. But I suppose an indoor pool is my real fantasy." She smiled. "Satisfied?"

Predatory eyes gleamed at her. "No."

"Taskmaster."

"I'd enjoy tasking you."

"Bleeding woman here."

"Shower sex—clean, wet, and warm."

"Wouldn't have thought of that." Her hands slid down to his butt. "What's your dream house, my Ian?"

"One with you in it."

❧ ❧ ❧

Before leaving for the island, Shannon called to check on Lizzie, described Ian's house, and told her of his plan to visit his friends.

"You just got back. How are you supposed to get ready for a completely different climate in a day or two? Let him steamroller you in the beginning, and he'll expect to always get his way. Bob tried pulling that crap. Bought a thousand-dollar crossbow behind my back. Believe me, I refused to let him live that one down."

Shannon smiled. Bobby had proudly displayed the bow in a glass cabinet.

Lizzie huffed out a breath. "Yeah, yeah, you don't see the point in holding a grudge."

"I just think refusing to forgive is like drinking poison yourself and expecting the person you're mad at to suffer. Besides, I'd hardly ever speak to my family if I held a grudge."

"You might be better off. I sure as hell don't miss that basket case of a sister of mine. I can't take her nonsense. Let people judge. They don't walk in my shoes."

Lizzie had prodded Shannon into her shoes, complete with excruciating details, many times. Shannon preferred to store hers safely out of people's way.

❧ ❧ ❧

Since the boys' father worked weekends, Ian asked Everett to supervise them during his and Shannon's trip to the island. The older man's stare pierced Ian. "Why the island?"

"To meet my friends, of course."

"Ian, you don't think—?"

"Doesn't matter what I think." His hand rose. "Sorry. Master Kai asked to meet her."

Everett fervently hoped Shannon was not the woman Ian and the Devoted had been searching for. He could not fathom such a destiny.

Ian told Christopher and Michael that Everett had volunteered to take care of them while he and their mom visited his friends. Since Everett cooked meals similar to the take-out foods they loved—he did not reveal the healthy ingredients he included in them—and told stories of his grandchildren, they had no objections.

Shannon's uncertainty over the trip lessened at her sons' easy acceptance. She had learned to rely on the strong intuition that guided her on who could be trusted. She trusted Everett and hugged him in thanks. He assured her it was not a problem, but she wondered about the worried look he thought he hid from her.

In bed the night before their departure, Ian stared intently into Shannon's eyes with something greater than passion rousing him. Wanting her had evolved to needing her, which instead of scaring him made him feel stronger and steadier.

Though unable to pinpoint what made Shannon more, he knew other people also responded strongly to her. In the pool at the resort, their fellow swimmers never noticed her when she did her exercises. The one time he saw her deliberately engage them, however, they thronged to her and entered a lively, yet friendly, exchange of ideas.

Ian's admin Charlotte, who wanted only a small circle of friends and rarely brought up his or her personal life, had offered Shannon friendship and had encouraged him to pursue her.

"There's something about that woman," Charlotte said, "that draws you to her."

Even Fran, a glass-half-empty type of guy with entrenched ideas, thought Shannon's environmental views more articulate than what the usual earthy-crunchy people—Fran's term—spouted and intended to look into some of the things she'd told him.

Ian and Shannon lay on their sides, and Ian pulled her against him to run his fingertips from her neck, down her spine and thigh, and back up while pressing his mouth to her forehead, nose, and cheeks.

"My friends are going to adore you," he said.

"And the older man, Master Kai?" Her body settled into his. "He seemed familiar, though I know I haven't met him, and he doesn't look like anyone I know." She shook her head. "Weird."

"In a bad way?" Ian asked.

"No, he feels more comforting than threatening."

"And fatherly, a good listener. I could confide in him that I didn't want to work in the family business after college. That caused—not a rift, exactly—tension between me and my father."

"I imagine Master Kai helped you realize that the tension on your father's side came from his disappointment in having to alter his dreams rather than disappointment in you."

Ian blinked. "What makes you say that?"

"From how you described your parents, I guess. I get this picture of them, arms around each other's waist—your mother in green slacks and a sweater, your father wearing a yellow shirt—standing on a little hill and smiling down on you."

"What do you mean, you get a picture?"

"It just pops into my head if I think about them."

Ian propped himself up on his elbow. "I don't remember showing you that picture."

Shannon shrugged. "Maybe you described it to me."

"Mm, maybe." Ian kept the picture in his office. He wanted to discuss Shannon's insights with Master Kai, so let it go for the moment. "Love, what about your parents? You haven't told me much about them."

She reached up to play with the small patch of curls on his breast-bone. "Different dynamic. My parents didn't involve themselves much in my life, which sounds neglectful, but I preferred being left to my own devices. I learned what I needed to know from books and my cats. I always had a cat to love."

Ian stroked her hair. "You can't have a conversation with one."

Shannon laughed. "Sure you can if you learn to speak Cat. I knew what they meant by their meows and purrs, how they rubbed against me."

"A cat whisperer, huh?"

In answer, she nuzzled his neck and purred. "Bet you can translate that."

"I love you, too." Ian kissed her and hoped she felt all the emotions overwhelming his ability to speak.

They talked some but mostly cuddled late into the night. When Shannon fell asleep, Ian simply watched her breathe and tried not to think that the island might change everything between them.

❧ ❧ ❧

The couple boarded Ian's jet at ten in the morning and, owing to the time difference, would land during the morning of the following day, a half-day flight.

"It's a long way to go for two days." Shannon gazed at the empty seats. "You don't have a smaller plane for two passengers?"

"Not one that would cross the Atlantic."

"Oh. Why not fly commercial?" She doubted that had occurred to him.

"The island has one airstrip. This plane is the biggest craft it handles." He didn't say so, but security precautions precluded commercial flights.

Ian worked on his laptop. After an hour of reading, Shannon rose to perform light stretches. She flowed from one graceful pose to the next. Ian especially enjoyed the ones where her ass pointed in his direction. Approaching her silently, he looped a hand around her waist and reached down with the other to tickle between her cheeks. She grabbed a chair arm.

"Is your flow still heavy?" he asked.

"No. I'm done. My period has gotten lighter and shorter as I've grown older."

"It's a good idea to nap, begin adjusting to the time change," Ian said as he slid his hand inside her pants and caressed over her panties from waist to crotch.

"I have difficulty napping during the day." Breathlessness lessened the ring of challenge in her voice.

"Let's see if I can provide a sleeping aid."

Ian made swift work of her clothes, unzipped his pants, and parted her knees. His hurry unnerved Shannon. He sat, pulled her backward astride his long legs, and pressed her torso forward until she had to grasp his thighs. A panicked little sound escaped her as hot, engorged flesh prodded against her labia.

"I've got you, baby." Ian parted her petal-soft folds and glided through their valley. He fondled her ass, his shaft pressing firmly on her clitoris with each pass.

Guilt at doubting him quickly ebbed as Shannon's hands clenched and unclenched on his legs. The different sensation sent a heavy, aching yearning deep into her belly. She rocked faster. Their climax burst convulsively, their bodies slowly returning to normal. Shannon's muscles suddenly went lax.

"Christ!" His heart jogging madly, Ian clutched her to his chest.

"Oh, wow. Sorry. Legs gave out. Did I hurt you?"

"No, baby. I was afraid of you being hurt."

"You saved me, my Ian."

His arms banded about her. "Hey, sorry I scared you." He eased his grip and captured her mouth in a possessive kiss.

Shannon peeked up at him impishly. "I'm really sleepy now." She landed across his lap to be paddled and tickled.

Ian kissed her cheeks, then set her upright to find her pants. Seats close together along one side transformed into a bed. Ian pulled out pillows and a light blanket from the overheads. He tucked Shannon in beside him.

After napping for a few hours, they washed in the restroom. Arms, legs, and torsos continually brushed up against each other. Ian lifted Shannon onto the counter and leaned on his hands. She traced the planes and angles of his face and kissed him affectionately.

"Want to join the mile-high club, pretty girl?"

"Didn't we already do that?"

"Only counts in the bathroom."

"Nut." She placed her arms around his neck. "You okay, my Ian? You seem a bit . . . desperate?"

"I waited a long time for my beloved." A warm rush of well-being soothed Ian's sore conscience at not disclosing the real reason for their trip. A tickling at the back of his mind suggesting he often felt a sense of well-being in her presence evaporated when Shannon locked her legs around his lower back. Their mouths and bodies fused in a slow and tender sharing. Lost in what he could give her, she let her head loll back. He loved her in every particle of his being.

❃ ❃ ❃

A bluish-black sea lightened to aquamarine at the coast of an irregularly shaped, lushly green island. The airstrip, dangerously narrow to Shannon's eyes, became visible. Ian warned her of the upcoming jolt from an unpaved, packed-earth runway, and she gripped the armrests.

They disembarked to a cloudless sky. The sun stung Shannon's skin, long covered against New England's winter chill. Ian hailed his waiting friends, and she watched the men embrace with an endearing lack of self-consciousness. She tilted her face to meet Lee's twinkling hazel eyes. Wood- and metal-sculpted animals and flowers ornamented thick chestnut dreadlocks loosely tied at the back by a leather thong. He had a strong-featured, unexpectedly pretty face.

Lee lifted her as he might a child to kiss each cheek. Shannon beamed unguarded, instinctively drawn to him.

Lee blinked and dragged his eyes away to sling her small duffle bag onto his shoulder.

"Packs quite a punch, doesn't she?" Ian whispered.

Liu inclined his head in a slight bow and kissed Shannon's cheeks. His willowy build intimated a greater height than his not quite six feet. His eyes brimmed with playfulness, and to his delight, Shannon unleashed her imp in kinship.

At five feet seven inches, Fael was, to Shannon's thinking, exactly the right size. His shoulder-length, sable hair brushed her face as he kissed her cheeks. An impulse to sink her fingers into the dense softness embarrassed her. Eyes that dominated over a sculpted nose and full lips ensnared her. She vividly recalled their mesmerizing glow.

Whipcord-thin, Fael grasped Shannon's hand. A sense of great strength flowed through her. Liu held her other hand and led her into the surrounding forest on a winding path. People of many races, some in cultural clothing including sarongs, turbans, and the head-to-toe abaya with most wearing loose, lightweight shirts and trousers, smiled in welcome, their eyes warm on Ian and resting briefly on Shannon before twitching away. Their body language suggested wariness, not distrust as much as a carefully dampened anticipation. *Weird*, she thought.

The group entered the center of the island's one village, a clearing where an open-air market paved in cobblestones took up most of the space. One-story buildings in browns and greens blended into the verdant perimeter. Shannon recognized sophisticated planning in the quaint design. Too many people gathered for introductions. A headache brewing above her eyes, Shannon gladly stayed in the background.

"Ian," said Liu, "let us bring Shannon inside to rest." She had turned pale.

Lee handed Ian her bag and said, "We'll see you at dinner." Fael nodded.

Ian and Liu escorted her to a guesthouse. The couple's room sat at the end of a hall. A door left open to the outside framed a garden of crushed rocks from shining quartz to granite chips artistically arranged around islands of flowering or leafy plants. Shannon hoped to explore it later. Their airy room included a bed adequate to accommodate Ian's length. Weary, Shannon wistfully eyed the bed with its exotic island-flower bedspread.

"I am a healer," Liu said. He lifted two glasses of a light green substance from a side table. "This should help to offset the jet lag."

Shannon sniffed, smelled herbs, and sipped. It tasted of melon.

Ian downed his. "If you don't mind, love, I'll visit while you rest. Say, two hours?"

"That'll be fine. Thank you, Liu."

He retrieved the glasses and bowed. Relieved to be alone, Shannon tried to shake the gnawing sense of something wrong and lay down.

❧ ❧ ❧

Someone sat on the bed. How long had she been sleeping? Groggy and expecting Ian, Shannon reached for him. A smaller, wrinkled hand met hers. She bolted upright.

An elderly man chirped cheerily. "I recognized you."

"Pardon?" Shannon backed off the bed. Frail, he offered no threat. But old memories lashed at her. She wanted out of the room.

"Ian brought you, a good man, his friends also." She nodded and moved cautiously. "He shall open you for the joining."

"Sorry?" Her stomach pitched. "I don't understand." Prayed to God she didn't.

He rose. "You have a fertility goddess's body, made for the art of pleasuring."

Shannon flung open the door, raced outside and headlong into a heavy mat of humid air. Rocks shifted beneath her feet. She fell hard on her hands and knees. Rolling to the side, she gulped for breath and fought the impulse to retch.

Get up. He's following. Cradling her hands, she struggled to her feet.

Alerted by someone, Ian rounded the building, his friends on his heels.

Shannon ran barefoot, straight toward jagged rocks. He shouted her name, his voice no match for the adrenaline roar of blood in her ears.

Ian sprinted, launched, and tucked Shannon safely within his arms and legs. Her body bucked with the strength of panic. He pinned her to the ground. "Shannon, stop." She wheezed brokenly. "I'm here, baby. What the hell happened?"

Lee squatted beside them. "Ian, your weight's pushing Shannon into the rocks."

"God. Sorry, baby." He carried her to a grassy spot under a tree and held her curled up against him. A group gathered.

Liu checked her feet. "Some bruising, no lacerations."

Fael gripped his arm. "No, she is in pain."

"Are you hurt?" Ian examined her legs to find bloody knees.

Liu asked someone to fetch his bag.

Master Kai arrived and nimbly knelt. "What happened, dear one?" he addressed Shannon. The elderly stranger who had followed Shannon shuffled up to the group. She curled up and trembled.

Ian raised stricken eyes to Master Kai. *What was going on?*

"Is the little one hurt?" asked the man.

"She has suffered a fall, Esias," Master Kai said.

"Ah, a shame if it interferes with the joining." He gave Lee's shoulder a friendly pat.

"Esias, have you been speaking to our guest?"

"We spoke of Ian's privilege to open her for his friends."

"Dear God," Ian whispered.

The man lurched forward and grasped Shannon's calf. Ian's chest muffled her cry. Master Kai carefully pried at Esias's fingers. He had a firm grip for one so frail.

A panting woman knelt beside the elderly man. "Abuelo, you should not disturb our guest. Come home now."

Esias patted her cheek. He patted Shannon's leg. "You shall accept these men."

Shannon flung herself to Ian's side and vomited. The woman grimaced in apology and led her grandfather home as he chirped happily.

Ian laid Shannon on some clean grass. "Baby." He felt like slime.

Shannon said faintly, "Sorry."

Liu, Fael, and Lee avoided her eyes. Ian's eyes darted away and broke her heart. Twinges of pain crossed her bone white face as she awkwardly rose to a sitting position. "Ian?" The haunted wisp of sound floated on the air. "Everyone's anticipation . . ." Her voice chilled and many in the crowd shivered. "For a public spectacle? Allow you easy access, so why not others?"

The men flinched at the slap, the sting worsened by the dead tone of her voice.

"Baby, I swear no one will hurt you." *What had Esias told her, for God's sake?*

Master Kai said, "Permit Liu to treat your injuries, dear one, and then meet the Council of the Devoted. We shall explain. Do not give credence to the ramblings of a man suffering from dementia."

"Excited expectation," Shannon said, "collusion—it pours off every one of you."

"Is she empathic like Fael?" Liu asked.

Fael shook his head. "Her abilities far exceed mine."

Master Kai interrupted. "A strong, willful, no doubt difficult woman, and a great blessing to her loved ones, yes?"

Shannon hadn't a clue what that meant, and *What is this dear one crap?*

Noting the cradled hands, Master Kai offered his. "Please."

After a brief hesitation she laid her fists in his hands. Her stiff fingers unclenched to gasps from the onlookers. A large patch of skin under the thumb of her blood-encrusted right hand flapped toward her wrist. Dirt and debris filled several cuts on her left.

"I cannot care for these injuries here," Liu said, voice harsh. "She needs the infirmary."

Master Kai nodded and rose in one movement. "Lee, please carry Shannon." His raised hand cut off Ian's protest. "Permit us to care for her. If her fear and anger rest on us, perhaps she may more readily forgive you."

Fael draped an arm over Ian's drooping shoulders. The gesture of support didn't help. The council was supposed to explain the true purpose of the visit to Shannon in a calm setting, tell her about the Devoted, and assure her she alone would decide whether to take the test that could determine if she was Jasirey. The plan ruined, Ian worried their relationship may have been ruined as well.

Expecting a fight, Lee cautiously approached Shannon. Worn-out, she made no objection, no sound, no eye contact. He'd have preferred a punch.

At the infirmary, Liu checked her vitals—mild signs of shock—then washed her knees. He doubted Shannon would accept sympathy for the pain she repressed. Having absorbed most of the fall with her hands, she breathed deeply as he cleaned them. Liu removed the skin flap, used glue made for flesh wounds on one cut, and bandaged the hand.

"Expect a raw soreness for a time." He numbed the left hand, sewed two jagged gashes closed, and dressed it. "The wounds are not severe, though they will affect your dexterity. Keep your hands immobile for a day or two. The knees received scrapes and bruises. Introduce movement after the swelling subsides and as pain allows."

The bandages alone rendered Shannon's hands useless. "And if I need the bathroom?"

Liu wished it was possible to erase the last few hours. "We have people to assist you." A few tears trickled down her cheeks. He blotted them and called in a female nurse to help her. He joined Lee who waited to carry Shannon to the nearby council hall.

"How is she?"

"Suffering considerable pain." Liu shoved a chair. Lee watched in concern. His friend rarely indulged in temper. "She seems a different woman."

"She's shut us out."

"No doubt." Liu pushed his hands into his pockets. "Why should it matter?"

Lee's smile failed to crease his broad cheeks. "You want her and wonder what you'll do if she doesn't accept you. I wonder the same."

"We have no proof that she is the one."

"Don't we?"

How Many Husbands?

Overhead fans in the council hall moderated the heat to tolerable. A large group of older men and women waited on floor cushions in a semicircle. Shannon tensed. Lee whispered encouragement and set her on a cushion before the council. On display and resenting it, she fought the impulse to curl into a ball.

"Thank you, Lee," said a woman wearing a dark head scarf. "We shall care for her."

Lee signaled Master Kai to follow him out. "Liu says she's in pain, exhausted, and emotionally stressed. He's sending a nutritional supplement with added pain medication."

"Thank you, Lee." Master Kai rejoined the council.

Many on the council wore the loose shirt and trousers that seemed to be an island uniform, but Shannon also saw a kilt, a casual jacket over a T-shirt, and a sundress.

The councilwoman asked, "What does Liu say about your injuries?"

Shannon shrugged. "Inconvenient. They'll heal." A man served tea and offered her a cup. She stopped herself from waving her bandaged and useless hands in front of his face.

A young man entered holding a light green drink. Master Kai took it and kneeled beside her. "You must be hungry. This may suffice for the moment." He lifted the straw to her mouth.

Silently, she cursed him. "It tastes different." Not a direct accusation.

"Liu included an herb to ease the pain. Do you find it unpleasant?"

Shannon finished the drink and, hoping elevation helped, drew up her stiff knees to rest her throbbing hands on them.

The councilwoman said, "Let us tell you why Master Kai invited you to the island. We call ourselves the Devoted. Those of us on the island

and others living off island, such as Ian, dedicate our lives to Jasirey, a woman destined to sow seeds of stability in a precarious time and bear children who will help bring those seeds to fruition."

Pretty name, Shannon thought blearily. She wanted to lie down.

"Jasirey steps forward whenever the world reaches a crisis point—historically, every three to four centuries. The name is more of a title, not the same woman each time, though many here believe in reincarnation. We all believe current global problems qualify for her to appear. Master Kai asked the council to interview you and decide if you should undergo a test we use to determine whether a candidate is Jasirey."

Shannon's fertile brain summoned a million questions and only one response. *Bullshit.* She left that unvoiced. "I assume candidates are just given superficial details."

"Understandably."

It irked Shannon that she couldn't point an accusatory finger. "I've been brought here under false pretenses, lied to. You need to understand I'm not feeling particularly cooperative."

"Events this morning—most unfortunate. Normally we broach our agenda under controlled conditions. We regret your pain and distress."

The woman's evident sincerity cooled the hot air in Shannon's balloon of resentment. "What did the old man mean?" Certain they'd heard the story, she didn't elaborate.

Master Kai said, "Esias spoke of a ceremony that occurs after a woman becomes Jasirey, when she chooses her husbands."

Shannon's head snapped up. "Husbands?"

A councilman smiled. "According to legend, the average number is fifteen. In this present age of instant communication, multiracial husbands will be required to father diverse children better suited to influence the many cultures of the world."

"The Devoted have existed for centuries," Master Kai said. "I am also a member of the Imperiat, a ruling body that collects and passes on the oral lore and written records of Jasirey to each generation. We tend the Imperiatu, a test for candidates. If a woman successfully passes the test, she then chooses her husbands from the Protectors of Jasirey, unmarried men dedicated to protecting her and possibly serving as husbands or fathers. The choice is always hers."

Though the men and women of the Imperiat maintained the Imperiatu and its mechanisms built centuries before the advent of computers, the knowledge of how it deciphered that a candidate passed or failed the tasks set before her had not survived the passage of time.

With a lot to absorb, Shannon focused on one salient point. "These men wait who knows how long, and if they do marry this woman, you expect her to keep fifteen guys happy?" A rumble of humor passed through the group.

"The Protectors vow to ensure Jasirey's happiness and well-being, a sacred duty. A bond with Jasirey is exceptionally profound. An elemental woman ingrained in the female, she never reincarnates as male, which provides a power and an allure critical to her success. She relies on her husbands' protection in various ways and their support in fulfilling her mission. A greater number secures her survival should any one husband become incapacitated or die. We prefer varying ages for the same reason. Long-lived, Jasirey conceives late in life and must pass on the unique attributes that enable her children to fulfill their destinies."

Shannon's aspect lightened. "I'm not her. It would take a lot of kids to influence every culture. I'm too old."

A woman wearing scrubs said, "One of many blessings bestowed upon Jasirey is the ability to bear healthy children beyond the normal fertility span."

Shannon persisted. "Unusual allure—I can count on one hand the number of guys I've dated. Even my ex-husband . . ." She shrugged. "I'm not this woman."

"Jasirey appears in middle age," Master Kai said. "Her allure may stem from maturity. Scarce information on her early years exists. Ian loves you."

She stared at the ground.

"Dear one," Master Kai continued, "Ian's vows to the Devoted dictated his duty to bring you to us. Though not easy for him, he will revise his dream of a wife for the greater good. Ian's friends are Protectors. You feel a connection to them, yes?" His eyes twinkled as hers, guilt-ridden, shot up. "This bolsters his courage."

The man's humor escaped Shannon. "Bet you're not supposed to influence candidates."

"If we influence or alter your decisions, you are not Jasirey. We live to serve her purpose, not to impose ours upon her."

"Uh-huh. I won't be bullied."

"I am pleased to hear it." Master Kai's head inclined in respect.

Shannon couldn't help liking the older man, and she could tell the others believed what they said. She needed more time to decide if she believed them, though she definitely did not think she was the woman they wanted. And if not, where did that leave her and Ian?

His distress under the tree had blasted through her own as his need to comfort her triggered a reciprocal need in her to comfort him. She wanted him beside her, believed he belonged there but, not inclined to rely on intuition, wanted to give it more thought when she had the energy.

She turned her attention back to the council and sighed. "I thought Liu was a healer."

"Yes," a councilman said. "Many of us acquire several affiliations. Lee and Fael are Protectors as well as skilled craftsmen and farmers."

"How old is Liu?" He seemed the youngest.

"Thirty-two, a median age for husband candidates." Shannon pulled back, and he placated her. "Jasirey chooses those she can love. A Protector desires nothing more."

"Protectors in training," Master Kai said, "are ineligible. Some, close to the age limit or facing reality rather than legend, may be disinclined to follow Jasirey off the island, leaving perhaps fifty candidates."

Shannon shook that off. It didn't pertain to her. Still, they had to expect her curiosity. "She doesn't live here?"

The woman with the scarf said, "Oh, no. For Jasirey to use her gifts, she must freely move through the world—interact with those whose minds she may influence. And to understand and continue their mother's influence on the world, her children must live with her."

Shannon frowned. "What gifts?"

The woman's eyes softened. "You have given us glimpses. Time shall be required to learn your full capacity."

"Seems an awful burden to put on children." Shannon rocked back and forth, unaware she did so, and the council recognized it as her coping mechanism for pain, unease, and flagging stamina.

"We ask nothing of the children until adulthood and encourage them to pursue individual paths. Their impact comes from their personalities rather than from whatever training we may provide. We always find Jasirey outside the Devoted."

Shannon switched gears. "Want to tell me about the test?" After attaining a consensus, the council described the Imperiatu as a type of maze or puzzle. Good. Puzzles weren't her forte. "What happens when . . ." If? No, be honest. ". . . when I fail?"

"The people shall be grateful for your attempt. We often call ourselves the people when referring to the whole."

Shannon debated with herself and decided taking the test hurt no one and would give the people closure when she failed. "I don't see the point, but if you still want it, I'll take the test."

"Thank you, dear one. Your ability to cope may be hampered by injuries. Master N'yu-wen shall examine you. She decides the opportune time." An elderly lady nodded.

Shannon curled around her knees. "Where am I staying in the meantime?"

With the perfect cue, Ian slinked in beside her. "Please, baby, return to the guesthouse with me." A glistening sheen in his dark eyes mirrored her pain.

Shannon wanted to whap him, but her arms automatically rose for him, a bodily knowledge akin to muscle memory that enabled her to trust and accept comfort from him despite the many questions whirling through her mind.

He gathered her in his lap. Relief shuddered through him as she clung and cried in her quiet way.

Master Kai placed a comforting hand on Shannon's head. "Care for her, Ian. She requires food, rest, and reassurance."

"See?" Ian's wet cheek rested against hers. "You told me everyone needs that. Please reassure me you still love me."

She pulled back, eyes on his chest. "Wrong question."

Ian cradled her face. "Not sure what you mean."

Shannon struggled to meet his eyes. "Did you pursue me for you or for the Devoted?"

"I love you, baby, loved you long before it dawned on me you might be Jasirey, which I'm afraid I'm still not coping with very well." Tearclogged noses interfering, they kissed in short sips. "I'll always love and cherish you, whatever your destiny."

❧ ❧ ❧

Shannon disliked feeling like an invalid as Ian trundled her to the guesthouse in a small cart. At their destination, tired and not thinking, she grasped the edge to climb out and hissed.

Ian carried her inside, placed her on the bed, and cupped her hands. "Are they bad?"

Shannon waved the bandages in his face. "They're useless, and I have to pee."

Ian burst out laughing at the picture of her coping with mummy-wrapped hands.

"Yeah, you can laugh. Wiping's no chore for . . ." She gave him a smug glance. "You have to wipe me, so there." When he laughed harder, she smacked her head into his chest. "Cut it out."

"Oh, dear God. Sorry." He wiped his eyes. "Sorry. Okay." Ian lifted her to her feet.

Shannon hobbled the few steps to the bathroom. Perspiration dotted her blanched face.

Ian grasped her elbows. "I'm sorry I laughed, love."

"Oh, shut up. I like your laugh."

Oddly effective as reassurances went, he wiped her and rearranged her clothing.

"This is humiliating." Shannon buried her face in Ian's shirt.

"I doubt you'd think so if I were the needy one."

"True, but you would."

Probably, he had to admit. He placed cushions on the bed and propped her in a sitting position. "The guys are bringing dinner and pain medication." Ian gazed into her hazy eyes. More than pain and fatigue distressed her. "Can you forgive me, Shannon?"

"The council said you acted out of duty. I'm not sure I understand."

"If Jasirey, your importance to the world far supersedes my needs."

"And mine? I want to marry you, not a bunch of strangers."

Ian winced. He had thought only of his feelings about Shannon being Jasirey, never hers. "Whatever happens during the test, you decide your future. No one forces you into anything."

77

"Makes everything my responsibility, but no pressure." Desperation laced Shannon's voice. "What do you want me to do?"

Ian bit back another futile sorry and gathered her close. "No matter how many others, my head trusts your love for me won't waver. My heart has no choice but to catch up." He laid a hand over her heart. "It lives here."

A knock on the door announced Lee, Liu, and Fael. Ian helped Shannon drink Liu's painkiller-laced smoothie. The three men stood, fidgeting.

Shannon blushed. "Guys, sit on the bed. Somebody has to feed me."

The men fed her chicken, rice balls, and vegetables. Fael gently applied a napkin as needed.

Shannon intently regarded the three. "You guys are Protectors of Jasirey. You'd really be content to share a wife, an older wife? You're all at least a decade younger than Ian."

Reverence radiated from Lee's eyes. "To hook our destiny to yours and your sons' . . ."

"*Her* destiny," Shannon interrupted, tangible heat blasting from her. "Not mine. Explain multiple husbands? We live in a provincial town. I won't subject my kids to censure on my account."

"Be assured," Fael said, "the Devoted have had centuries to evaluate every contingency and to formulate ways to protect our most precious lady and her children."

Shannon relented at the earnest plea in his eyes. "I said I'd take the test, but no other promises. My sons come first."

"Understandable." Liu signaled the others to desist. "We shall leave you to rest."

Lee bent to kiss her cheek, and having no idea what prompted it, Shannon angled her head to meet his lips. Both started at the instant sizzle. Furious color suffused Shannon's face.

"Gentlemen," Ian said quietly, "kiss the lady good night."

Shannon wilted, wishing she could disappear under the bed. Lee finished their kiss, lips gently molding hers. Liu pressed tenderly against her mouth. Fael wrapped around her and imparted a passion that scorched her nervous system. The men left without a word.

Ian's arms circled Shannon's cringing body. She burrowed into him. "You're bright as a flame, love. Did the kisses feel wrong in the moment?"

He cupped her face and watched realization dawn. "Everything's all right."

❧ ❧ ❧

The next morning, despite Ian's nonchalance at cleaning her bottom, Shannon's tears trickled down her cheeks. His hand running up and down her back comforted her. He returned her to the bed and fed her fruit and yogurt topped with chopped nuts.

Shannon made a face at her bandaged hands. "I have to call work. I hate having to renege on the two-week notice I gave them."

"Injury is hardly reneging, love. Ought the boys to stay with Everett?"

"Roger's nights off are Tuesday and Wednesday. They stay with him those two days. Do you think we'll be here that long?"

"What did the council say?"

"A Master New . . . something or other decides when I'm ready to take the test."

"N'yu-wen."

"Right. Couldn't Liu examine me?"

"It's probably an internal to determine if you're ovulating."

Shannon stilled. "What's that got to do with the test?"

"Uh, well, a woman undertakes the Imperiatu during ovulation. If Jasirey, she undergoes the husband ceremony. Once chosen, they consummate their relationship. I thought the council related the whole story yesterday."

"I suppose . . . what the hell do you mean, consummate?" Ian's eyes crinkled as she worked it out. "Jerk, I can un-choose you, you know."

He smiled smugly. "Feisty female, aren't you? Because you've already chosen me, I'd be a husband-protector and stay at your side."

"And watch. Pervert."

A steely glint shone in his dark eyes. "Not quite a voyeur, interesting as that might be." Though trained and disciplined, the Protectors would find Shannon—a living, breathing Jasirey—a tempting morsel. A gentle thumb erased her worry lines. "The husband-protector ensures the candidates maintain strict protocol."

"So, if I'm her and choose fifteen—"

"Or thirty."

79

She glared. "These guys . . ." Her voice rose on each word. ". . . at the same time?"

"Hardly. Biology requires one at a time." Ian stopped teasing as, eyes wide, she shook her head. "It's an ancient, controlled, and respectful ceremony. Jasirey's body sustains less stress throughout than in one bout of our sexual exploits."

"Ian, I can't. This isn't me." How could he expect her to agree to that?

"You wouldn't be consciously aware." Ian blamed the council for her what-the-hell? expression. "Cultural conventions tend to override one's intuitive knowledge. An herb is used to sedate Jasirey and thereby increase the likelihood of choice without prejudice."

"I would think consciousness a prerequisite to any choice."

Ian forged past her acid tone. "Closer to a twilight sleep, the subconscious is free to respond. The husband-protector watches for signs and signals the accepted candidates."

"Ian, you describe this weird ritual as if it's run-of-the-mill. Then what? She brings however many home with her and lives happily ever after?" Talk about forcing drastic changes on her sons. Shannon saw no alternative but to fail the test.

❦ ❦ ❦

With Ian's help, Shannon called work to explain that injuries from an accident would prevent her from returning home when planned and working out her notice. They understood and wished her well. She made arrangements for the boys to stay with Everett when their father was at work.

Liu tended to her wounds each morning. Shannon's swollen knees prevented exploring, so she looked forward to stories from Liu, Lee, and Fael about their training as a team under Ian and as Protectors. It surprised her that Ian had started out as one.

"The majority of Protectors are male," Fael said, "to give Jasirey an optimal number of options for husbands."

"Females go through the same defensive and offensive training as we do," Lee said, "but don't need the sexual know-how or understanding of the female mind."

Liu smiled as Shannon made a sound suspiciously like what Americans called a raspberry. "Males and females communicate differently,"

80

he said blandly. "Males tend to view others' comments on their stories as competitive posturing while females usually comment to show sympathy or solidarity."

Shannon snuggled into Ian. "Maybe you should have continued your training."

"Mm, nothing competitive about that statement." Ian nuzzled her neck. "Bet you don't have any complaints about my sex training."

"Why don't females need the sexual know-how?"

Lee picked up one of her bare feet and began massaging it. "They won't be Jasirey's lovers. Sex training only addresses ways to please her."

Shannon's eyelids began to droop. "No LGBTQ Jasireys, huh?"

Liu picked up her other foot. He lightly scored the sole with his thumbnail, which jolted Shannon back to full wakefulness. "Not so far," he said, eyes glittering with suppressed laughter.

"Women," Lee said, "volunteer to help teach us about the female body and psyche."

"Seriously?"

Fael managed to maintain a sober mien. "Such instruction takes place in the second year of a Protector's training. I, for one, shall always be grateful for the lessons."

No one mistook the sound Shannon made then.

⚜ ⚜ ⚜

Master N'yu-wen set an appointment to examine Shannon. She and Ian slowly walked to the infirmary in the temperate morning air. Her stiff knees loosened. Dangling, her hands ached more, so Ian had fashioned one sling for both arms. Curbing their excitement, which saddened Shannon, people they met on the paths greeted the couple. She hated to blunt anyone's hopes.

Master N'yu-wen waited for them in the exam room. "You appear rested," she said to Shannon. "At the council hall, we believed you were at the limit of your endurance and left the tale unfinished. I assume Ian remedied that. Undress her from the waist down."

Ian lifted Shannon onto the table and covered her with the cloth the healer handed him. Two narrow arms protruded from the table's front end for the feet. Ian guided Shannon.

"We dislike the restrictive use of stirrups," Master N'yu-wen said.

The arms moved to the table corners and effectively parted the patient's legs. Shannon failed to see the improvement. The brusque healer's hands were gentle and swift. Ian helped Shannon shift up the table for Master N'yu-wen to remove the bandages.

"One to ten, quantify the pain," the healer said.

"The hands ache," Shannon said. "The knees are sore. Liu's herb drink helps."

"Obviously such wounds hurt. I asked to what degree."

"Compared to what? I can walk now. I still can't use my hands."

The healer's brow lifted. "You find the inconvenience more bothersome than the pain?"

"No point in complaining if it won't fix anything."

"Ian, her stoicism may challenge you. Consider it a natural trait rather than a lack of cooperation." Leaving Shannon's fingers free, the healer dressed her hands. "The mucous is fertile. The test must be conducted tonight."

The mucous—what? "And if this puzzle requires hands?"

"I cannot advise you. I am on the council and not privy to the mysteries of the Imperiatu." Shannon stared as Ian bowed to the older woman's departing back.

Ian dressed her. "We bow in respect to leaders, especially after a service has been rendered." Shannon pointed to the sling. He realized her hands hurt. "Let's find Liu."

Shannon's smoothie in hand and practically bouncing, Liu stood outside the door. "The Imperiat commissioned me to care for Shannon. They wish to impart instructions to you." Liu leaned in. "A Protector's take? She is ovulating. Lovers remain off-limits until after the test."

Turning imploring eyes on Ian, Shannon whispered, "Don't go."

"The Imperiat wants to explain my duties for the ceremony. It's tradition."

"They won't appreciate me, then. I'm not big on annoying traditions."

Ian kissed her and waved before disappearing round a bend.

❧ ❧ ❧

At the marketplace, Liu pulled out a bench from a shaded table for Shannon. Yellow-veined, thick-leaved plants separated the tables from the food vendors and Shannon from prying eyes. The people's anticipation weighed on her. Liu noticed Lee and Fael at one of the stalls and gestured to them. The men walked over to hug Shannon and kiss cheeks blushing a softer pink than any of the surrounding flowers.

Empathic, Fael engaged the mental blocks he'd been taught to guard himself from others' turbulent emotions and, at the moment, against the flood of nervous confusion from Shannon. "The test causes you anxiety. We shall consider it our job to divert you." And, in the process, he hoped to divert himself from the nearly overwhelming urge to protect her.

"Master N'yu-wen couldn't describe the Imperiatu," Shannon said, "because she's a councilwoman. Imperiat, council, Elder—what's the difference?"

"They are all masters in their fields," Liu said, "or gifted in wisdom. The people choose the Elders, who lead the island. The council chooses members for itself from the Imperiat and Elders, has the final authority in any disputes between the ruling bodies, and manages Devoted businesses, aid missions, and general security."

"Imperiat members believe themselves called," Fael said, "and oversee matters and missions related directly to Jasirey—the Imperiatu, the Protectors of Jasirey, her safety."

"What missions?"

"We can explain that at a later time." Lee speared a glance at Fael and Liu.

"Secrets, maybe Ian commanding you guys in undercover work?" Ungracious but, figuring it was their turn, Shannon enjoyed watching the men squirm.

Lee gathered the remnants of their meal. Liu brushed at crumbs. Unsure of Shannon's intent and eyes molten, Fael dropped his blocks and probed. He sensed nothing darker than female versus male mischievousness and disparaged himself when her eyes flew to the ground, lips parted at the shock of the mental intrusion she felt but did not understand.

Of more concern, Fael sensed a strength in her so great that, had she gone on the offensive instead of backing down, he might have been dropped to his knees. She required training. He doubted she recognized her own potential.

Shannon turned to Lee. "Were you born on the island, Lee?"

"No, my family came from Samoa." Lee slid an appraising glance over Fael, whose glowing eyes cooled, head wagging in remorse. "Polynesian but including Dutch and German ancestors. I'm the middle kid of two more boys and two girls, all of us young when the Devoted recruited my parents for the three sons eligible to train as Protectors and for my father's wood-carving skill, or so I thought.

"We're Jewish. Over ninety percent of Samoans are Christian, the religion brought into coexistence with fa'asamoa—the traditional Samoan way—based on the principle of vafealoa'i—relationships between people based on respect. Samoa has a rich mythical history that includes intricate tattooing. Jewish religion forbids tattoos. It set us apart and concerned our parents. They later told us that besides wanting to be part of Jasirey's mission to better the lives of all people, they also wanted more options for our futures.

"My older brother and sister returned to Samoa at maturity and lead happy, productive lives. My younger brother moved to Germany to work in a Devoted computer firm. My sister Beryl stayed. All married and have made me an uncle many times over."

Shannon realized that as a Protector, Lee had no children, nor did Liu or Fael. It seemed weird, maybe even wrong, but she couldn't pursue the thought. Bodily functions took priority. "Liu, you deal with people's bodies. Guess you get bathroom duty. Sorry."

Fael and Lee wished her luck on the test. Back in her room, Liu cooled her flushed face with a damp cloth. "Adjusting to the island's climate takes time."

Shannon gave him a rueful smile. "It surges from comfortable to soggy in the passing of a cloud."

Liu switched on the overhead fan. "Rest. I shall check on you later." He turned down the bedding and removed her sandals. She glanced at the door. Liu squatted to her eye level. "You are safe. Esias meant no harm. His granddaughter watches him."

Shannon thanked him and lay curled up on her side. Liu feared tears rather than sleep. Maintaining a good distance between them, he removed his shoes and lay behind her. She peered over her shoulder.

"I am caring for you as promised. Sleep." Liu rubbed her tense back.

"Ian cuddles close."

"Do not tempt the poor male."

She apologized, her voice suspiciously mirthful, which did not assist him in relaxing.

"Why'd you come to the island, Liu?" His accent suggested he hadn't been born here.

"From a young age I recognized my gift for healing, first animals and then people. My parents encouraged me to seek training, though we had no money for universities. They and my father's two younger brothers run the family farm in a rural village of China. I left to find someone to apprentice me in Chinese traditional medicine—a holistic approach to healing that concentrates on prevention and balance among bodily systems.

"To this day, I have kept in mind advice from Li Shizhen, a sixteenth century physician. He wrote, "To cure disease is like waiting until one is thirsty before digging a well."

Shannon thought that was a simile worth committing to memory. "How long did you travel?" she asked.

"For three years I learned about acupuncture, reflexology, and herbal medicines while supporting myself as an itinerant healer. Then I met a recruiter who recommended me to the Devoted. Here, I added training in the western healing arts as well as in defense. I am included on missions as a healer. And that should suffice to lull you to sleep."

Liu slept and woke instantly when, dreaming, Shannon snuggled into him. Not meaning to wake her, he inched back. A sleepy smile curved her lovely mouth. Liu twined fingers through her hair, brought his mouth to hers, and ran a hand down her spine. Back arching, Shannon molded against him. Liu released her mouth with a slight pop and jumped off the bed, bending forward to force blood into his head. Sitting gingerly, he patted her hip.

"My head is reeling." His eyes glinted. "Yours?"

"Doesn't hit me there." Her eyes the color of the sea danced.

Liu rumbled in his throat and plucked her from the bed. "The healer prescribes exercise."

They walked along shaded paths and for cover during a five-minute downpour sheltered under a tree, its lower branches trained together. With low-hanging, sheltering branches, similar trees dotted the path.

"Can you explain why the Devoted recruit people?" Shannon asked.

"We search for Jasirey and those potentially useful in serving her mission."

"Which, according to the council, is to have kids who help the world."

Liu considered what he might safely divulge. "Jasirey sets the stage for the children. Her . . ." He decided against gifts. Shannon clearly recognized nothing special about herself. "Her personality and the state of the world determine the details."

"The council also mentioned reincarnation," Shannon said. "I had a Hindu friend in college who believed people achieved a higher or lower status in the next life depending on their conduct during their current life. Many gods connect to an ultimate power. I forget the name. I've no idea how Buddhism differs."

"Brahman is the Creator in Hinduism. I am neither Hindu nor Buddhist, though duty to and acceptance of one's position in traditional Chinese society are similar, perhaps less restrictive. The Chinese Communist Party now allows more religious observance. Though it is strictly regulated, religion has become quite popular again. The Chinese people do, however, tend to define you according to your birthplace. Wherever I traveled on my quest, people first asked from where I hailed.

"Here I have studied various religions. The historic Buddha described nirvana, the final goal of a person's journey, as complete peace, needing nor wanting anything. In China, Buddhism was sometimes adapted to include the strong Confucian bonds of family and society and an afterlife."

"But they view spirituality as a solitary journey, no gods, right?"

"In simple terms, Buddha taught that cravings for the pleasures of this world cause suffering. Release the cravings, relieve the suffering. Obtain enlightenment through the eight-fold path that includes right views, resolve, speech, conduct, and livelihood as well as replacement of ill will, malicious talk, lust, and harm to living things with mindful concentration through meditation." Liu squinted, counting off on his fingers. "Not quite right. Some pieces belong together. And yes, nirvana is gained on one's own, no intervening higher powers. The cycle of rebirth stops, though one may choose to stay in this world to guide others."

He was awfully cute. Shannon suspected that, for Liu, teaching ranked close to healing.

A woman approached. "Liu, Master Kai asks you to escort our guest to her room and join the Protectors. Someone shall transport her to the Imperiatu at the proper time."

He thanked the woman and returned Shannon to her guest room. "I wish you well in your task. Try not to worry."

❧ ❧ ❧

Crying to relieve her tension required blowing her nose, which required hands and meant burning pain, which sucked. Shannon breathed in slowly to the vision of hearts and flowers—love and thanks sent to heaven—and breathed out as a glittering light beamed down to fill her. In her mind holding a ballerina pose, her body gracefully twirled to dispense that loving light to others. Silly maybe, but she felt better. She drifted in and out until a knock at the door fully woke her.

A woman wearing a gold-trimmed turquoise sari carried in a basket. "I am Tiyah, here to dress you and bring you to the Imperiatu. I also have your dinner and medication."

Shannon's stomach churned. Prepared for a nervous candidate, Tiyah offered bland banana slices and roasted chicken before laying out an opalescent short-sleeved robe. Beaded at the waist, the top layer of beads—the deep blue of the sky after a storm—trickled down through a royal-purple midsection to form pools and rivulets in the summer-green bottom layer.

"Jasirey's signature colors." Guessing by Shannon's reaction, she said, "Your favorites as well?" Shannon nodded. "The robe suits you. My family worked the beading."

Shannon examined them. "It's stunning. There must be hundreds."

"Thousands, actually. Your appreciation will please my mother and daughter. Come. Time to prepare."

Tiyah removed Shannon's T-shirt and shorts. Carefully slipping the robe's sleeves past the bandaged hands, Tiyah fastened a single closure at the waist. The robe draped perfectly, no gapping at the bust or leg. Tiyah brushed Shannon's short waves to a silvery gleam. The women went out the front door where a horse-drawn cart waited.

His throat contracting rhythmically, the driver stared at Shannon. Tiyah clipped out something in, maybe, Hindi. The young man steadied

Shannon as she stepped up to a seat, assisted Tiyah to her seat, and then swung himself into the driver's seat.

A hint of the day's heat remained, the air scented with flowers. A gossamer slice of moon stood sentinel over wisps of clouds bathed in tangerine, coral, and pink. The cart trundled into the cooler forest that shut out the glorious display. Goosebumps formed on Shannon's bare arms. Before long, the hum of voices swelled louder than the whir of insects.

The sound abruptly ceased when the cart jostled into a clearing and drew alongside a low platform. Thirty feet back, thick forest nestled along its sides. A heavy curtain crossed the stage there, hiding its depth.

Wearing a knee-length, sapphire robe tied at the waist, Ian stood next to a short set of stairs. He held out a hand to Shannon. "You look beautiful. Doing okay?"

Shannon thanked Tiyah and the driver and said, "I thought I'd be alone."

"You tackle the Imperiatu alone. I stay on the stage to monitor your progress. We need you to describe everything you see and feel, okay?"

Shannon nodded, somersaults in her stomach expanding to cliff dives.

On the stage, Master Kai and several Imperiat and council members welcomed Shannon. A mown meadow in front of the stage accommodated a sea of hushed people. Master Kai cupped Shannon's elbow to bring her center stage. Darkness descended and the lights above the curtain switched on. He spoke in English while translators interpreted in various languages.

"For some time, the world's need for Jasircy has markedly grown. We thank Shannon for assenting to undertake the Imperiatu and pray wisdom be granted to her."

People on the stage placed a hand at Shannon's waist. She couldn't move. Ian locked eyes to calm her. Master Kai prayed in singsong, a pretty cadence. In a language unknown to Shannon, the people in the audience chimed in at prescribed intervals. She realized the Devoted took it all seriously and wished she had an alternative to dashing their hopes.

Council and Imperiat members retreated. Ian said, "Baby, to go through the Imperiatu, you cannot wear anything that might become tangled. You leave the robe behind." A shudder coursed through her. "Your underwear isn't much different than a bathing suit."

Ian had informed Master Kai of Shannon's shame-based modesty. They agreed on swift action to prevent fear from debilitating her to the point of shutting down. Ian pivoted her toward the audience. "Tell them what you choose to do."

Her mind jangled. *Quit. You'll disappoint them. Won't go naked.*

Sympathetic calls asked what upset Shannon. Her voice barely carried. Those in front repeated to those behind. "I can't do this—undress in public."

"Yet," a man said, "the lights show your body clearly in that sheer robe."

Several yelled, "You are lovely."

Shannon gaped and looked down. "Then this isn't see-through."

The people laughed and clapped. Ian knew Shannon was dead serious. Taking advantage of her confusion, he stood behind her, unfastened the robe, and pushed it off her shoulders to pool on the floor. She whirled, stepping closer to him.

Ian pressed his lips to her forehead, then knelt to remove the bandages at her knees. He stood to undo those on her shaking hands. Bright lights glared on the raw, unfettered wounds. The people's noises of sympathy brought a tremulous smile to Shannon's drawn face.

The curtain began to part with a low rumble. Body rigid, Shannon turned. A two-story cube the width of the stage and embedded with sapphire, amethyst, and emerald stones glowed and beckoned. She swayed forward, everything else forgotten in an urgent compulsion to go to it.

Ian grasped her shoulders. "Remember, tell me everything you experience."

Her arms squeezed his waist, and Shannon walked toward her destiny.

<h1 style="text-align:center">The Imperiatu</h1>

Expecting to feel cold stone, Shannon instead felt warmth emanating from the cube and heard a faint, not mechanical tonal hum. She rested her cheek against the stones.

The audience suppressed a collective indrawn breath. No other candidate in the people's memory had shown such visceral connection to the Imperiatu.

Shannon peered up at the cube. A slight wavering or haze caught her attention. She angled her head to the left and stairs appeared. Righting her head made them disappear. Cool. "See the staircase?"

Stern gestures from Master Kai hushed the audience's excited murmurs.

"No, love, I don't," Ian said, sounding strangely happy to Shannon.

"It's an optical illusion," she said. "Am I allowed to climb it?"

"You decide your course but continue to describe what you experience."

The stairs started on the left. Small knobs—handholds, probably—dotted the wall at each step. Shannon felt safe despite the sheer drop on the right. To the audience, she appeared to be walking on air. The stairs ended at a small landing. Shannon scanned the Imperiatu for more clues. A noise below drew her attention.

"Ian, the steps are sliding into the wall. If this landing disappears, I have nowhere to go."

Hands clenched, Ian stood quietly.

An unnatural square-shaped amethyst caught Shannon's eye. She pressed her fingertips into the stone. A rod emerged above her head and released a harness. The step beneath the landing moved. Quickly examining the harness, she pushed her arms through what she assumed were armholes. A fastening clipped behind, but she couldn't manage it with her injuries. She hadn't time to turn it around as her feet backtracked on the receding landing. Legs dangling, she grabbed the harness.

His feet fixed to the floor, Ian watched Shannon's swinging, barely tethered body.

Shannon used her arms to clamp the harness to her torso while sucking in deep breaths to relieve excruciating pain in her hands and slow her pounding heart. She searched the wall. On the left where the stairs had begun, maybe six feet above where she hung, a ledge jutted.

"There's a ledge. I don't know how I'm supposed to reach it." She strained to hold on.

"Shannon, do you . . . ?"

"Let me think." Some of the stones protruded more than others. She stretched a foot toward one, and it pulled on the harness. The rod inched forward. *Yes.*

It was a short-lived moment of relief. The harness was meant to free the hands for climbing. She grasped the stones with her stubby toes. Climbing upward frustrated Shannon to the point of tears. She resorted to using her knees, scraping the scabs off on the stones and leaving a blood-smeared trail on the cube.

Ian called soft encouragement. Shannon's focus and determination amazed him.

Shannon concentrated on deliberately placing her burning knees. Her lungs labored. Her underwear plastered to her overheated skin. Having lost any sense of time, she neared the ledge. A few stones allowed her to climb higher and ease onto it, but Shannon was done. She swung her legs, built momentum, and thudded onto the ledge like a beached fish. The people winced empathetically. The rod retreated and dragged the harness from her inert body. She gulped harshly for air and raised a trembling forearm to wipe sweat from her eyes.

"Talk to me, Shannon."

She batted at the air and said, "Leave me alone." Nervous titters sounded in the audience.

"Baby." Ian's gut churned at the agonizing impotence of his role.

"No, not you," she murmured. "It wants something, goading me." A few repetitive notes of the humming cube drilled into her head, then swelled and twisted in intricate patterns of a song. "Okay, it's nice now."

Or was until the compulsion to sing along struck her. In Shannon's view, singing in public deserved the same ranking as being naked in public. Humming burred inside her, insisting that she follow the melody. Shannon sang wordless sounds in a high, pure tone.

Enchanted by the angelic notes, onlookers momentarily forgot the test. Ian wondered what other surprises his sturdy, courageous woman held in store.

As the song ended, a small rectangular box emerged from the wall slightly above Shannon's head. Light glittered along a pathway of purple stones on the box. Her fingers traced it to the back. "There's an opening. I need to check if anything's inside. This better not hurt."

Ian smiled at Shannon threatening the huge Imperiatu.

At an awkward angle, she raised her right arm and crooked the elbow to reach. Advancing inside the box by fits and starts, she encountered only smooth surfaces. Not entirely unexpected, the box pressed in and held her encased hand immobile. Infuriatingly, something stabbed into her wrist. Shannon's upper body flung forward and back again at another stab.

"Shannon, what's happening?"

"It's hurting me." She rapped the box hard with her free hand and bruised her knuckles. Pissed tears scalded her cheeks. Another stab. "Stop it."

"Baby, listen to me. Lie down."

Ian sounded far away. Her head hung heavy on her neck. *Did he say, "Lie down"?* Shannon dropped, banging her head. Too worn out to fight, she wondered, *Why wouldn't the wretched thing let go?*

The box flipped upward against the wall and dragged her encased hand above her elbow. The crowd erupted. Lines of blood streamed down her inner forearm.

"Shannon, are you all right?"

"Hurts. Squeezing." The blood flow lessened and soon stopped. "Something gloppy." The translators stumbled on gloppy. "Hot now."

The box released her limp hand and receded into the wall. Sleep pulled at Shannon, but the song called. *Had it stopped before?* She examined her hand. *Ooh, pretty.* An oval ring, a long opal embedded in amethysts, sapphires, and emeralds, covered her middle finger to the central knuckle. Five fine chains fanned out from the end to a wide etched band around her wrist glistening with a thick ointment. Snug with no clasp, the gold bracelet obscured the puncture marks.

Shannon raised her hand to show Ian. An explosion of cheers registered as white noise to her clouded mind. Master Kai, face creased in joy, contained the people's celebrating.

The Imperiatu permitted no time to rest. The top and lower third of the ledge receded and forced Shannon, fighting lightheadedness, to sit upright. Stone knobs rose on either side of the seat. She grasped them as the landing vibrated and moved swiftly toward the center of the wall. Pain in her hands cleared her head a bit.

Below, a hole in the stage opened and enlarged. What resembled a large aquarium full of water rose, one side nearly flush against the wall. The ledge stopped above the tank, tilted, and dropped Shannon. She pulled her arms and legs into a ball at the water's stinging impact, but the viscous fluid soon soothed rather than hurt. Shannon drifted, listening to the song reverberating pleasantly through the warm liquid.

The people held their breaths. Their most precious lady unfurled, kicked off the bottom that lay ten feet from the surface, and breached. Arms outstretched, she paddled her feet to stay afloat, a brief interlude. Water swirled, carrying her to the middle and becoming turbulent.

The tank bucked and pitched. The audience jumped to their feet to cry out a warning as a thick wave slapped Shannon from behind. She sputtered after a second to her face. Her legs flew out of the water, and her head pushed beneath the surface.

Shannon hit bottom, scrambled to get her legs beneath her, and emerged to a mouthful of water. Her arms flailed as she was thrown into a wall. She fought for a deep breath and submerged. Beneath the surface, the water bubbled whitely but not wildly.

Shannon had never liked the sensation of being under water. She couldn't breathe to calm herself. She forced herself to look around and get her bearings. She saw a hazy ring on the wall abutting the Imperiatu. Swimming to it, she reached out and touched a metal rim with a latch she assumed was a port that opened to a passage.

Should she trust that the passage would lead to air quickly enough or rise for a breath and risk being slapped down by the waves again? Opening the port would allow water to fill whatever space lay beyond. Shannon sensed it led to safety. She didn't know. She did know the Devoted cared about her well-being. Lungs rebelling, she pulled. The door didn't budge. Her vision blackened. Shannon pushed and was rushed out of view.

❧ ❧ ❧

Ian shouted again for Shannon. The Protectors eligible for the husband ceremony stood ready at the stage steps.

Master Kai said, "Ian, please continue calling."

Three more shouts, and a wavering voice answered. "Don't yell. Dark here."

She wheezed like the broken accordion Ian remembered once finding in his grandparents' attic. "Baby, that scared the hell out of me. Shannon? Don't go to sleep."

Wet but not cold, she sprawled face down on something soft. She shifted onto her back. The same colors as her new ring, a small cluster of lights floated above her. She described them for Ian. A circular area brightened around the lights, and a darker shape swooped in.

"Ian, it's you, my bald eagle."

Grateful her voice sounded less strained, the people murmured approval of the strong spirit.

"Think an eagle has pale skin under its feathers?" Shannon asked.

The legendary traits of Jasirey included the ability to recognize her husbands by animal spirits, one of the clues that had pointed to Shannon being Jasirey.

Right then, it hit Ian that Shannon would now be known as Jasirey. He let the joy of finding their lady overwhelm his regret at having to give up Shannon as his fiancée alone.

"Here comes Lee, such a sweet teddy bear," Jasirey said. Well, a great brown bear."

An apt spirit for Lee, it surprised no one.

Jasirey watched as something thin and cord-like came out of the eagle and brown bear and attached to the cluster of lights. "Huh, wonder what that is."

"Describe it," Ian said.

"Strands of some sort flew from you guys to the lights, connecting you." Jasirey wasn't sure how, but she realized that the pretty lights were one female being.

94

"And here comes . . . must be Liu. He morphs back and forth from a stodgy badger to the playful, clever ferret. Hope he chooses the ferret. Uh, am I supposed to say that?"

Ian's heart swelled with affection.

"He'll figure it out," she said. A strand bound him to the light.

Liu and Lee slapped each other's backs.

"Whoa, Fael's a viper. Gold eyes—hard to look away—dangerous."

Her startling pronouncement caused a twinge of guilt among the people, who teasingly called Fael, with his unusually long tongue, Frog. Liu and Lee, witnesses to their friend's capabilities, acknowledged the aptness of the fierce spirit.

Jasirey's unexpected laughter intrigued the people. "Four threads floated up from the light," she said. "A small opalescent light is forming at each end."

Master Kai cradled his arms in the age-old sign for a baby. The Devoted bowed their heads in deep thanksgiving. Their lady would bear more children.

"The colored light looks ill. It's fading, disappearing."

Ian's hands flew to the back of his neck. "And the babies?"

"Babies?"

"The smaller lights."

"Really?" Jasirey said. "Finished growing, I guess. Their threads disconnected. The strands to you guys seem thinner, droopy. You're moving away. No, don't leave her."

The plaintive cry ripped at Ian, Lee, Liu, and Fael, though they knew that to answer the prodding urge to protect her would interfere in Jasirey's vision.

"Okay, the light's getting brighter. The strands are becoming strong again."

The people sighed in relief.

"Good," she said. "You shouldn't be separated. It was killing her."

Knowing Jasirey's vision was a premonition of things to come, her men each felt a cold shudder.

Jasirey watched as — *seriously?* — a wild boar led four flitting, formless shadows in charging the light to hurl short strands that penetrated it. In her weariness, unable to decipher this confusing jumble, Jasirey remained quiet. Then she recognized a second set of opalescent little beings.

"Five more lights. If they represent babies, that's an awful lot of kids."

Ian's fist pumped. He grinned at the whooping and cheering people. Master Kai waved insistently, but his beaming face lacked its usual authority.

An amorphous dark hole opened in the light. Since the colors didn't fade, Jasirey said, "She doesn't seem as ill this pregnancy. The little lights are breaking off to stand next to the other babies."

She remained quiet for a time. Then, "Ian?"

Her wavering voice grounded him. "I'm here, love."

Cold penetrated her bones. Dark red, burnt orange, and muddy yellow oozed and melted into thick sludge, garish colors then leaching to drab lifelessness.

"Baby, what's happening?"

She yelped, and the people braced. She laughed, and they breathed.

"Lights switched on. Closet of a room. The floor lowered, and I'm caught in a strappy thing hanging from the ceiling, maybe a sex swing. For guys with bad backs? You should see it."

"I'd like to," Ian said. "Can you guide me into the Imperiatu?"

"When have you ever had trouble finding your way inside?"

Face burning, Ian endured the whistles and catcalls. "Jasirey." He used her new name and let a little sternness into his voice to help her focus.

"Who? Oh. Her. Me. You mean me?"

"Yes, you, our most precious lady."

"Serious. Takes the fun out of it."

Ian felt he just needed to keep her focused a while longer. "Jasirey, do you see a map?"

"Uh, okay. You still on the stage?"

"Yes, of course."

"Snippy." She described a series of stones in front of a door.

Following the walls, Ian sprinted through the trees, found the stones, and tried numerous combinations. "Love, I'm not getting this. Do you see any other clues?"

"I think it wants you to sing. Oh, yeah, you don't sing." She wanted Ian. "Purple, blue, purple, green, purple."

"Got it." A doorway opened to reveal a narrow passageway. It seemed to wind through the Imperiatu for some distance, and Ian wondered how many rooms it held. Finally, he heard Jasirey singing softly. He entered a small room.

She smiled dreamily at him. "Hi, my Ian, which do you prefer?" She indicated her spread-eagle pose. "Or . . ." She tried flipping to a backside view.

She perched precariously on the straps, and Ian's firm hand stilled her. He looked predatory, sexy. Dropping his robe, he stood naked and at full alert.

"I want you any and every way, my beautiful girl." Ian turned off the room's microphone and slowly peeled off her bra and underwear while securing her in the straps.

"I want you, too, just plain Ian."

He smiled in fond memory of their first time. "I must prepare you for the ceremony, Love."

"Okay." Whatever that meant, she didn't care. She needed him.

Ian tipped the swing over, slid a hand down her back and over her ass, then stood between her drawn-up knees. He massaged her shoulders, back, and thighs. It pleased him when Jasirey didn't flinch as he drew soothing circles around her waist. He loved every inch of her and hoped maybe she had begun to believe it. No doubt the drug administered by the Imperiatu helped.

Ian nipped Jasirey's ass, knelt, and steadied her using a hand on the joining of hip and leg. In no hurry, he applied lavish strokes of his tongue through Jasirey's valley until her fragrant heat bathed his mouth and chin.

He stood and lifted her hips to the required angle, slowly sheathed himself as she opened to him, slid out on a moan at her tight caress, and drove in. He buried himself again and again to the echoing slap of meeting bodies.

Jasirey moaned, close to a whimper, and writhed against the tethers. Ian's name on her lips, she begged him, her pulse raging, his wild plunging roaring through her, sending pleasure flaring in brilliant streaks of light.

Clutching Jasirey's hips, Ian bucked and shuddered until, body quivering, he collapsed. He caught himself on the swing's straps and rested his head on Jasirey's soft cheeks. His breathing labored at a gallop. When he recovered sufficiently, he turned her and grabbed his discarded robe to blot perspiration from her rosy body.

"Baby, did I hurt you?"

Sex-hazy eyes adored him. "My Ian, my heart."

"I love you. I'll get you something to drink."

Instructed by the Imperiat to find the box holding the potion for the husband ceremony that would put her into a twilight sleep and prevent societal or cultural prejudices or fear from interfering with her choice of husbands, Ian took in the room as he closely searched the walls. *No maps. How had she guided him to the door?*

Ian found the box. He opened it and removed a goblet and two bottles. Pouring the contents of the smaller bottle into the goblet, he hesitated. *Ought* he *to give her all of it?* The Imperiatu had overmedicated Jasirey when she struggled against the injections. It was too late to ask for advice. Her welfare rested in his hands.

Ian poured a third of the liquid back into the bottle.

Ian lifted Jasirey's head and held the goblet to her lips. He felt a twinge of guilt at her unquestioning acceptance. Her pupils dilated, and her eyelids drooped. She breathed peacefully. His lips brushing her forehead, Ian prayed for guidance as her husband-protector. He shrugged on his robe before checking her raw hands and knees. No bleeding. Ian turned on the microphone and informed the Imperiat that Jasirey was ready for the husband ceremony.

The Imperiatu creaked as a small door retracted into the cube to leave an opening not visible to the audience, who would only hear Ian proclaim whether Jasirey accepted a Protector.

Led by Master Kai, the Imperiat waved incense and chanted prayers for the well-being of their revered lady and her children born and yet to be born. After asking for blessings on Jasirey's choice of husbands, they retreated.

Master Kai remained at the door to usher in one Protector at a time. Charged with being bodily ready, if accepted, to consummate their relationship, each approached, shed his robe, stood between Jasirey's thighs, and leaned over her—a symbol of his protection of her—to kiss her forehead, eyes, and heart. The ceremonial ritual ended mouth to mouth. If their lady responded, Ian allowed the accepted man, who also had become Jasirey's husband, to enter her, leave his seed, and stand next to him for the remainder of the ceremony.

Lee, Liu, and Fael started the ceremony in the order Jasirey had specified. Lee stepped forward, mind centered on the woman before him, the tiny fulfillment of years of training, missions, and hope. He braced himself on the straps binding her arms. Praying they bore his weight, he banished the horrific image of his bulk crashing onto her.

Still reeling from Jasirey having already picked him, Lee began the ceremonial supplication, perhaps lingering a bit longer than strict protocol outlined. Her scent had him throbbing.

Ian watched to ensure proper conduct. Jasirey remained unresponsive. He worried she might be overly sedated.

Though not protocol, Lee lightly caressed Jasirey's cheek with his and murmured, "I love you." He molded his full lips to hers. Her calves rubbed against his thighs.

Ian grinned. "She accepts you." He poured the flask of lubricant on Lee's impressive manhood, hesitated, and added a bit more.

Unable to see her exposed, vulnerable sex past his erection, Lee almost lost heart. A glimpse of desire-glazed eyes, so brief he might have imagined it, nevertheless banished his fears. "Little one," Lee murmured, cupped Jasirey's hips, and lifted her to meet him.

Determined not to hurt her, he entered inch by fraction of an inch. *Dear God, the tight, wet heat of her.* He breathed to slow his thundering heart. She moaned softly, arched her back, and caused his undoing. A strangled roar, unrecognizable as his own voice, escaped him. Supporting himself on the straps, he carefully withdrew.

Ian choked back laughter at his massive friend transformed into a limp rag. He nudged Lee's head between drawn-up knees. Checking on Jasirey, he saw no sign of distress.

Liu approached and whispered, "I love you, precious one." He reverently followed the protocol. Jasirey's ankles lifted to rest on his hips before the kiss.

"She accepts you." Ian poured lubricant on Liu's smaller but no less adequate erection.

Liu refused to be denied his kiss. "Precious one," he said, slanted his lips over hers, and entered smoothly. Enthralled, he wished to stay forever embedded in her sweet body. Ian cleared his throat. Liu flexed his hips. Jasirey tightened around him, and he let go. He required a moment to center himself before handing a sheepish Lee his robe. He stood beside Ian.

Jasirey's legs embraced Fael the instant he approached her. Ian cocked an eyebrow. "She accepts you."

Fael efficiently fulfilled the ritual. Lingering at her mouth, he whispered, "Most loved one." Straightening for Ian's libation, he grasped her hips and stroked in, pressing against her clitoris. Jasirey sighed. Fael climaxed and, eyes molten, joined the other husband-protectors.

The people knew the four friends would care well for their lady. The ceremony, however, had just begun. A monotonous line of candidates followed, a far greater number than Master Kai had predicted. Few of the eligible Protectors opted to be released from their vows. They found Jasirey's shy warmth and remarkable smile intoxicating. Hopes high, they presented themselves one by one.

Jasirey remained oblivious until a mixed white and Asian young man with fair skin and tawny hair knelt beside her. Carefully clasping her injured hand, he said, "I am Kimika and unworthy." Better men than he had approached and left unaccepted. Trembling, he at first failed to notice the slight pressure of her fingers.

"Not a husband, but you're mine," she said in a faint voice, "my white lion."

"My lady." Offered an unprecedented mandate, Kimika bowed in veneration. He saluted Jasirey via their traditional yin and yang symbol—right hand palm down, fingers curled over the tips of curled left fingers, palm up. "My life belongs to you and yours."

Recruited at sixteen, Kimika exhibited a gift for creating stratagems useful on missions and in businesses owned by the Devoted. He grabbed at the Devoted's invitation and promise of acceptance. One of many multi-racial people on the island, he seemed eager to blend in rather than stand out. His induction into the Protectors of Jasirey surprised most.

Used to the people's affectionate but exasperated looks as he often stumbled through his tasks, Kimika vowed to live up to the respect and awe they showered on him as he descended into the crowd.

The Imperiat listened in wondering silence. The herb for the vision quest and prophecy would have subsided. The further proof of Jasirey's prescience exceeded their expectations.

Jasirey remained quiet through a series of candidates. One broke protocol when his hands inadvertently fell on her breasts. She uttered a frightened cry, raising her husbands' hackles. They grabbed the man and forced him away. Struggling to curl into a ball, Jasirey fought the straps. Master Kai took charge of the mortified candidate and ordered the men to care for their wife. They dropped at her sides to soothe her with calming hands.

The next candidates strictly followed protocol until one knelt to deliver the formal change of mind. "I am not yours."

"Why are you here?" she whispered.

"I am Mtombe, lady. I . . . I am not yours."

"Go find your path."

Mtombe hovered in disbelief. Free that easily? He reverently kissed Jasirey's hand.

Unable to fathom the meaning of this dismissal, the crowd murmured. People like Kimika and Mtombe, not born on the island, underwent a painstaking probation period. Once accepted by the Devoted, only a small percent changed their minds. Divulging their knowledge of the Devoted to outsiders rarely happened, and few had sufficient knowledge to be a threat.

Mtombe's great grandfather had been recruited and brought a family along. The children returned to Gabon upon maturity. His father worked for the Lope National Park in central Gabon as a janitor to the Mikongo research center that also had facilities for tourists.

Mtombe had hoped to become a park ranger, but his father, denied membership himself, decided one of his four sons should join the Devoted, a society he revered but knew little about. Despite Mtombe's upfront declaration that he applied out of duty to his family, the Devoted accepted him. His vision quest suggested a strong connection to Jasirey, hence his induction into the Protectors.

Possessing valid papers from a recent mission in London, Mtombe packed his few belongings and arranged transport. Later, he'd face going home.

The final candidates received no response and completed the ceremony. Master Kai led the husbands who carried their robed wife before the stunned people. Only four. The Imperiat chanted traditional prayers of health and fertility for the new family. The crowd stood to bow to the former Shannon. They would view and address her forevermore as Jasirey. How long it might take her to think of herself as Jasirey remained to be seen.

The husbands wheeled their wife in a cart to a one-room cabin containing a kitchenette, living area and, dominating the space, a bed adequate to accommodate the newlyweds. Lit candles sat on end tables at either side. They laid Jasirey in the middle and took a moment to admire their lovely, amazing wife glowing in the candlelight.

Liu tended her hands, stitches still intact. Lee and Fael placed ice packs on her bruised and swollen knees with a pillow beneath while Liu ensured her safety.

Deciding to let her rest, the men gathered on the small patio where, as their commander, Ian gave thanks for Jasirey's success with the Imperiatu and for her choice of husbands.

"We received an overabundance of training," Fael said. They had long studied the psychology and protocols for living as many men and a wife.

Ian frowned. "It's difficult to hide your feelings from her. I hope my . . . less than enthusiastic attitude didn't sway her to reject other husbands."

"The sedation," Liu said, "prevented logic or fear from interfering in Jasirey's choice."

"Such a whirlwind of events," Ian said. "There hasn't been time to share much about her. We've been together barely two weeks. I loved her the moment she smiled at me."

"That smile packs a hell of a wallop," Lee said.

"Yes, yet she has no clue of her sex appeal. She wants you three but may believe you want her only as Jasirey." Ian smiled as Lee's brow furrowed. "One life-changing event after another will be — is — overwhelming. Before me, she had one sexual relationship, her ex-husband. She believes he neither loved nor wanted her. She was overweight a good portion of her life, directly related to the insecurity about her body and, if you judge from the encounter with poor Esias, a possible protection from older male attention."

Fael's eyes flashed. "You believe someone molested her?"

"Shan . . . Jasirey rarely discusses her past. Master Kai said it's a reasonable hypothesis."

Lee growled. "Reasonable. Good thing the pervert's probably dead."

Ian laughed. "Sorry." His hand mock erased his reaction. "Not funny."

"What do you suggest for convincing Jasirey of our love?" Liu asked.

"Take it day by day. I think she puts more store in actions than words."

"Shall we live in your Boston house?"

"Too small, and Jasirey prefers the country. I purchased a farm on the outskirts of her hometown. The foundation and basic structure of the house are sound. Redesign of the interior has begun."

"I suggest planning a walled compound," Fael said, "and using our construction people to ensure security." He and Lee headed security for the Protectors of Jasirey and since recent developments, for Jasirey, her sons, and her other eventual children. Ian asked them to coordinate plans with Everett and the Imperiat.

"What else?" Lee asked.

"She's adept at hiding her feelings, more habit than deliberate secretiveness. Still, she can strain your patience."

"To chastise her over an ingrained trait," Liu said, "would delay her acceptance of the safe environment we wish to create."

Ian's eyes softened. "She told me she hoped I'd be her safe place."

"Yes," Fael said, "what we all must be for her if we wish her to confide her feelings and past reasons why she felt constrained to mute them."

"Tell us of her sons." Lee smiled at the affection lighting Ian's face.

"Christopher and Michael have their mother's smile and sometimes irreverent sense of humor, intelligent. Shan . . ." Ian shook his head. "Jasirey worries for them, but I think she'll have greater trouble accepting her role in the Devoted than the boys will. She's always loved and nurtured them, given them the ability to trust."

Liu stretched. "Let us rouse our sleeping beauty. She requires food and fluids."

Their wife curled on the large bed. Ian caressed her gleaming hair and the gentle rise of her cheek. She rolled onto her back. Ian's mouth brushed slightly parted lips until she responded, murmuring his name. Drowsy eyes fluttered and attempted to focus.

Liu sat beside her. "How do you feel?"

"Okay, I guess. Fuzzy." She sat up, grabbed for the sheet, and immediately unclenched her stinging hands. "I'm in this see-through thing." She spit it out like a curse.

Lee grinned and lifted her from the bed.

Her knees felt two sizes too big. Ian assisted her in the bathroom. She whispered, "What happened?"

Ian's mouth opened. He shook his head and carried her back to the main room. "Gentlemen, we're idiots. Our wife asks what happened."

"Poor darling." Liu hugged her. "What do you remember?"

"Jumbled pictures. It's hard to think."

"The drug shall dissipate by morning." He cradled her right hand. The brilliant gems of her ring flared against the white bandaging.

"Jasirey's bracelet," Lee said. Hands clasped in the Devoted's yin-yang symbol for her, the men bowed.

"You shall receive this salute," Fael said, "the sign of respect for Jasirey, from everyone on the island."

"They think I'm her."

"Yes," Liu said, "our most precious lady, and we, your husbands."

Fingertips picking at the sheet, she said, "After the Imperiatu, I agreed to continue?"

Lee, Fael, and Liu looked to Ian for context. Did she refer to the husband ceremony?

With greater understanding of her ambivalence, Ian waited for her mind to settle.

"Aren't there supposed to be a bunch of you?"

Fael blocked his feelings. He sensed Jasirey blindly probing at their psyches. Their vows precluded allowing their desires to taint her judgment. She had the right to renege on the marriage should she wish. "You chose four."

"Oh." She didn't voice her vast relief. Lee, Liu, and Fael's anxiety cut through the fog. "I'm sorry," she said. "I don't mean to hurt you. I'm a little confused."

Lee restrained the urge to reach for her. "Little one, we are yours and at your command. Your needs and wishes come first."

"Whatever time you require," Liu said, "you shall have."

Ian propped her up on pillows. Lee placed finger foods on a tray while Liu helped their wife hold a glass of his restorative minus the pain medication, her system soothed with sufficient drugs. She ate on her own, and the delicate ivory tone of her skin returned.

The men endeavored to act normally. Despite how unreal the night felt, she would follow their lead while trying to digest the idea that she was Jasirey. She studied the bracelet. The etching resembled the swirls of the beading on her robe. "Pretty but no clasp. That box zapped me enough times to get it on."

Ian's arms twined about her. "It was a rapid version of the fasting and meditating the Devoted employ for vision quests."

"Why didn't you tell me?"

"The Imperiat explained it to me after I left you."

"It hurt almost as much as that horrible climb."

"It applied a heat retardant to weld the band to your wrist. I feared it overmedicated you, incapacitating or, worse, setting you up to be injured." Ian rubbed her shoulders. "Tackling the wall—and the tank." He shuddered at the memory. "I was terrified, hated not being able to help you. Afterward, the Imperiat explained your adrenaline rush from fighting the water lessened the drug's soporific effect but enhanced its hallucinogenic properties."

"Now I know why drugs never appealed to me. Really don't appreciate anyone else drugging me, either. I chose to climb the wall. The tank scared me." Jasirey wanted to cuddle but refrained in front of the others. "The tunnel brought me to a room. I remember lights." Not ready to relive the parts of the dream or whatever she'd had that confused or troubled her, she quieted.

The men had been warned not to question her regarding her vision.

"Master Kai and the council wish to talk to you tomorrow," Liu said.

"Goody." Amused sympathy overlaid wariness in the men's eyes. "You came in, Ian. I lay on, uh, . . . and you, . . . we, . . . well, you know."

"A sex swing you called it, and we certainly did." He nuzzled her ear.

She blushed. "My memory's fragmented after that. Hey." She searched his face. "You drugged me, too, didn't you?"

"It was part of the husband ceremony." Ian refused to feel guilty.

Fuzziness returning, Jasirey sighed. "So, you four guys saw me in that contraption, and we . . . " Embarrassment and the lack of memory frustrated her. "But no others?"

"Would you like others?" Ian smirked at her glare. His friends would become accustomed to their wife's stubbornness. Her unacknowledged love for them and her strong sense of duty would bring her around.

Fael heeded Ian's advice and acted. He pressed his lips to Jasirey's, felt her body begin to succumb, and accepted it when she pulled back. "Thank you, beloved, for choosing me. I am yours always. I love you."

Lee tilted her face with one large finger to gently lay his lips on hers. "I am yours always. I love you, little one."

Eyes sparkling, Liu leaned close. "I choose the ferret."

Remembering that part, Jasirey smiled. Liu's sparkle darkened.

"I am yours always. You are most precious to me." His kiss mirrored the sentiment.

The men watched Jasirey mask her uncertainty behind an impish light.

"Doesn't seem fair I can't remember you guys naked."

Liu ignored his tightening loins. "Something to remedy at another time. Rest tonight. Your body has undergone sufficient stimulation for one day."

None of the men considered it necessary to tell her how many others had seen her naked in the sex swing.

An Unorthodox Family

Jasirey woke in the pearly light of predawn. The unfamiliar breathing she heard disoriented her. Images of the previous night swam in and out of her consciousness and nudged her to full wakefulness. The sight of all four men in bed with her sent a wave of anxiety crashing through her. She scooted on her bottom toward the bed's edge and bit back a yell when Lee lifted and held her face to face.

He nibbled, flicked the tip of his tongue over her ear, down her neck to her shoulder, and back up. He whispered, "Are you opposed to making out?"

Jasirey mutely scrambled for an answer as full lips caressed hers and huge hands roamed her curves.

Fael granted Lee two minutes. "Gentlemen, someone has appropriated our wife."

Instantly alert, Liu and Ian dropped on Lee. Fael grabbed Jasirey. Her surprised yelp fizzled into a squeak. The men orchestrated an intricate battle for their lady's favor, bombarded her sensibilities, and overrode her fear. One suitor bodily removed, the others charged in to kiss, fondle, or tickle in a playful cycle.

Jasirey laughed till she had to pee. Finding herself at the edge of the bed, she jumped off and stumbled, her knees stiff. Ian slung her over his shoulder.

After helping in the bathroom and returning her to the bed, he said, "Gentlemen, what do you think might be our wife's pleasure?"

Jasirey protested playfully, though not sure they were kidding. "Don't I get a say?"

"No," they said in chorus. Gentle hands anchored her to the mattress and lazily stroked her body. She turned pink but permitted it.

"Sex details belong to the discretion of the husbands," Liu said, "to prevent you from having to mediate any problems among us."

Ian wagged a finger at her. "So be quiet like a good girl."

Jasiery stuck her tongue out at him.

Fael smiled at the playfulness and looked forward to forming a similar relationship with her. "A husband-protector's responsibility always begins with your needs."

She sensed his earnest sincerity. It touched her—and incited her imp. "So, if I want just you for a month, everyone would agree."

Fael's eyes glittered. "I did not say your desires would always come first."

Ian captured her mouth. She twisted away. "You might get divorced before you even get married, buster."

Ian answered with a wicked smile. "I believe I've been threatened. I say we jump her."

"You'd squish me."

"A happy death."

Her laugh died at the carnal intent etched on their faces. "You seriously mean all of you?" Her voice rose on a faint whisper. "At the same time?"

"Our training was thorough, little one. We won't hurt you."

Fael wielded his tongue in a diverting kiss as the others removed the robe. Jasirey's tiny nipples hardened beneath Lee's and Ian's tongues and nipping teeth. Setting Jasirey on her side facing him, Ian raised her knees. Liu fitted himself behind her, parted her labia, and entered.

Pleasure simmered through them in each slow coming together and sliding apart. Liu came quickly to place a minimum of stress on Jasirey's body. Ian seamlessly replaced him, flexed his hips, and pushed her to climb higher. He pressed a hand to her vulva and applied light downward pressure. Hips grinding together, they hit the peak and plummeted to a blissful release. Ian cuddled a moment before Lee dragged their wife under his body.

Senses dazed, she weakly pushed at his chest. "Trust me," he murmured. "Let us show you your full sexual potential." The love and desire in Lee's eyes seduced her. He entered, filled every nook and cranny, and slowly rocked.

Leaving Jasirey on the brink, Lee quaked at the force of his climax. He groaned but moved aside for Fael to continue the insistent barrage to their wife's senses. She rose and fell in frantic need beneath Fael's striving body. He crested, meeting her liquid release with a fiery eruption. Her knees slid down to the bed, Fael collapsing to her side.

Being aroused and brought to peak more than once amazed Jasirey. She might still be a bit loopy but decided being Jasirey had its benefits.

Lee drew her into his arms. "Go back to sleep, little one."

The men hemmed their sleepy lady in a cocoon of warmth.

The men woke long past dawn. Reluctant to disturb their exhausted wife, they left a note on the refrigerator and walked to the training center for showers and breakfast.

> *Dearest Love,*
>
> *We went to the training center to let you sleep. Cut-up food and your medicated drink are in the fridge. There's a dress in the closet, underwear in the top right drawer of the wardrobe. Late morning, someone will escort you here to meet us. We love you.*
>
> *Your Husbands*
>
> *(Doesn't that have a nice ring?)*

Jasirey found the note, hugged the small piece of paper, and tucked it into her underwear drawer next to the piece of amethyst Ian had given her. Needing a shower more than food, she removed her bandages and entered the walk-in stall with multiple showerheads. A loofah on a stick worked well, though her hands stung after using it.

A lightweight lavender dress hung in the closet. V-necked and sleeveless, it had a full skirt, beading at the waist comparable to the previous night's robe, and no zipper or buttons. The bust contained built-in support. Wrestling the dress into place hurt, but the comfortable, flattering fit pleased Jasirey. She gingerly applied sunblock, then gratefully drank the pain medication.

Going out to the patio, she snacked on pineapple chunks and nuts. Rising humidity heightened the scent of orchids that grew on many of the trees shading the cabin. She took a break from thinking by bird-watching instead, a favorite pastime. Small, brilliantly colored lorikeets abounded. A flash of white feathers may have been a cockatoo. She watched spellbound as a group of fruit bats flew high overhead.

Finished eating, the reprieve over, Jasirey tried to remember what landed her in such a life-altering position. She had not intended to interact with the Imperiatu. The Devoted would no doubt say that God or fate intervened to ensure she met her destiny as Jasirey. She practiced breathing exercises to help lessen her anxiety.

At the inkling that someone was watching, her eyes flew open. An ebony-skinned woman with cropped hair, large hoops in her ears, and an elegant, long neck curled her fingers together in the yin-yang symbol and bowed. Jasirey returned the salute.

"I am Amador, here to lead you to the training center and your husbands." She smiled mischievously. "You need not return our gestures of respect. It would take you all day."

Amador caught sight of Jasirey's bare hands and clucked at the raw wounds. "Let us replace your bandages before we go."

Amador distracted Jasirey from the pain she caused her. "Not long ago, I worked with your husbands in the Central African Republic where I was assigned before coming back to the island to teach new recruiters. Good men, they saved several children from a human trafficker."

"They and you." Jasirey's sea blue eyes twinkled. "I suspect you used those earrings to good effect."

Amador recognized that the warmth and approval rushing through her came from Jasirey. With wonder, she also understood that their lady *saw* the role she had played in the rescue.

Moving at a pace to accommodate Jasirey's slower gait, Amador led the way to a wide path that wound through trees foreign to New England and fields smelling of manure and turned-up earth, a comfortingly familiar scent to Jasirey.

Numerous paths crisscrossed, a challenge to Jasirey's memory. They passed many smiling people who clasped their hands and bowed. Jasirey understood Amador's warning that there would be insufficient time to return all of the salutes. She settled for returning people's smiles.

They exited the forest to an open lawn dotted with training areas and, back near the tree line, the largest building Jasirey had yet seen. Inside the training center, Amador led her to a spacious, sunlit room that smelled not unpleasantly of human exertion and disappeared before Jasirey remembered to thank her.

Men and women stopped their training to bow. Feeling exposed, Jasirey searched for Lee, the tallest of her husbands. The four men sparred near one of the huge windows. She watched their focused moves and countermoves, highlighted in the streaming sunlight.

Lee flipped Ian to the matted floor. He nimbly regained his feet. Fael sent a side kick past Lee's guard. Lee blocked the next two. The men stopped a hair's breadth from contact—her men. "I am yours," they had said, the one thing so far that felt real and absolute to her.

The men saw their wife. Male smiles intensified as they took in the curve-flattering dress. Jasirey's stomach fluttered, and her eyes darkened. Oblivious to the gaping people around them, they swept Jasirey off her feet for good-morning nuzzling.

At a soft sound behind them, the men set her down. Smiling, Master Kai gave Jasirey the familiar salute. Bandages interfering, she merely bowed. His hand lifted to deter her.

"Don't," she said. "I'd like to return the salutes."

The building quieted. Even though she was Jasirey, the people weren't sure it was permitted to interrupt the head of the Imperiat and a council member as venerated as Master Kai.

"I understand tradition doesn't demand I return the gesture," Jasirey said, "and time often prevents it, but it seems wrong, arrogant, or rude somehow not to if I can. Is it such an important thing?"

"Your wishes take precedence," Master Kai said. "We are at your service, Jasirey."

"Not what I meant. Makes me sound like a feudal lord. Besides, everyone here has learned the legends of Jasirey and knows more about the concept than I do."

"You are she, yes? Who would know her better?"

Jasirey acknowledged his cleverness with a nod but persisted. "It's all right to return the gestures?"

"As it pleases you, Jasirey." Accustoming himself to her flinch every time she heard the name, Master Kai would nevertheless use it along with everyone else to help her adjust.

"The council wishes to discuss last night's experience," he told her. To the men, he said, "We shall lunch at the outcrop. Come for her in two hours."

The pair walked through dense trees that blocked the warming sun. Cool and dark, the forest seemed restful rather than creepy to Jasirey.

Winged insects buzzed. None seemed inclined to bite, and their song lulled her hovering anxiety.

"My husbands told me something of the Elders', Imperiat's, and council's roles. They mentioned that the Imperiat are called. I wondered what that means."

"Always curious. We believe ourselves mandated by a higher power to further your mission. Our one desire, to be in your service. You may have noticed a disproportionate number of men on the Imperiat. Many first served as Protectors."

The idea of so many ordering their lives for her benefit discomfited Jasirey, but the smell of wood smoke and sandalwood incense announced their destination. They entered a shaded clearing. The council sat on tiered stone benches carved from a crescent-shaped ledge. A cushioned rattan chair rested below for her. The leaders stood and bowed. She returned it with a firmness that demanded no arguments.

They glanced at a pleased Master Kai and rejoiced in their Jasirey.

A middle-aged couple served tea, flat bread, fruit, and kebabs from a table near a stone fireplace. The woman placed a plate of food cut into bite-sized pieces on Jasirey's lap. "You can manage, precious lady?"

Jasiery started at the accolade that somehow seemed worse than being called Jasirey. "Thank you, this is fine." She mustered her nerve and stood to command the council's attention. "Liu told me you want to discuss last night. Before that, I require a promise."

The council murmured. One said, "What do you wish, Jasirey?"

"I was given a hallucinogen without my knowledge." Her eyes fired. "I understand the purpose but don't ever do it again."

"Dear one," said Master Kai, "the herb has no side effects and is not addictive. It was necessary but will never be so again. You have our promise. Please eat. Do you like lamb?"

Despite no apology, Jasirey sat and popped a bite into her mouth to acknowledge the promise.

The council asked if she'd spent a restful night. A quiet radiance transformed her troubled countenance along with a full-blown grin and a furious blush. Then she laughed at herself. The council, pleased at a sign of acceptance, laughed with her.

"We understand," said a woman, "your body recovers and your spirit searches for its new place. We shall endeavor not to fatigue you. A point of hesitation occurred during your vision. We believe something happened that you did not tell Ian. As caretakers of the people and Jasirey's mission, that critical information would prepare us for whatever lies ahead."

Jasirey stretched her uncomfortable knees. "I intended to fail the test to prevent putting my sons in an uncomfortable position."

"Explain, please."

Sensing no annoyance from the group inclined Jasirey to be forthcoming. "I should have ended it and refused to climb the stairs. It sucked me in."

"The Imperiatu called to you, yes?" Master Kai said.

"You mean the song?"

"Partly. You also felt a connection to the Imperiatu, drawn to explore, did you not?"

"I did, but stranded in the halter, I can't imagine why I continued instead of insisting on a ladder. The climb hurt. I wasn't even drugged yet." She eyed the council to be sure and decided, no, she hadn't been. "Later, in the small room, the things I saw were hard to figure out."

"Exactly the reason we wished to speak to you now," a man said. "First impressions present a truer picture of the experience. Before we get to that, though, we require a decision. You are Jasirey. Nothing alters that fact. You alone choose whether to walk away or to accept your husbands, your people, and the responsibilities inherent in the role."

Jasirey breathed deeply to slow her rapid heartbeat. *Their expectations,* she thought. *They ask a lot.*

"Jasirey," Master Kai said, "we have made painstaking preparations for you. Trust us and your husbands to place your welfare above all else."

Husbands. Everything came down to them. The one clear and unassailable fact? Ian, Lee, Liu, and Fael belonged to her. Loving them happened in a heartbeat. The thought of relinquishing them gave her heart a painful squeeze. Jasirey leaped and took her men's word concerning their feelings for her. But involving her boys was another matter.

"What about my sons?"

"They are part of you, part of us. Our desire and duty to protect them equals yours. We are equipped for the challenge."

Keeping her husbands felt right. Jasirey also felt the conviction of the council's beliefs and such hope that she couldn't help but be moved—and swayed—by them. Either the Devoted would solve her misgivings regarding her sons or she would. Their welfare would always be her priority. She took another leap of faith and chose. "I'll be your Jasirey and do my best to learn how."

"Thank you, most precious lady." The council stood and bowed.

Master Kai continued. "It shall take time for you to determine your path and what assistance you will accept from us. Today we prefer to concentrate on last night. We believe your recitation of events was complete until you recounted the second pregnancy. What happened before that?"

"The colored light represented me?"

"Not a surprise to you," a councilwoman said. "Please describe the following events."

Jasirey rubbed between her eyes. *Concentrate.* "Shadows but no specific shapes like my husbands' . . . except for one, a wild boar that led the shadows."

Intending to mask the sudden tension in the group, Master Kai said, "It stands to reason that people have more confidence in others like themselves. Your children shall influence many peoples in our diverse world. You chose few husbands. It presents difficulties."

"You're saying I have to choose more?" Jasirey blushed at the squeak in her voice.

"You may or you may not. Jasirey often consorts with various suitors to ensure the diversity of her children."

Prudent for the moment, the council did not mention that Jasirey usually saw the spirit animals only of her husbands.

"Come on. You expect my husbands to say, 'Sure, no problem. Take other lovers.'"

"They understand the requirements of your calling. So, after the quintuplets' birth—"

"The little lights in my vision, four the first time, which you're saying are kids, and then five the next time. Do you realize the strain of a multiple pregnancy on a woman? Especially an older woman. And you expect me to do it twice?"

"While not recommended for the average woman, Jasirey is blessed. It has been foretold. It shall be." Intending to help her acclimate, the council switched between addressing her directly as Jasirey and using the name impersonally.

"Nine children. You realize how old I'd be before they graduate from high school. At my age, people start planning for retirement, not which diaper to use." Several of the women chuckled.

"You have your husbands, your own considerable strength of will, and the people for any support required in meeting the challenges you face. Please stop evading the question."

Jasirey rested her head on sore knees. The chill from the previous night permeated her senses. Master Kai descended to lend his steady warmth.

"I can't tell you much," she murmured. "Fiery colors but freezing." Master Kai patted her back. "I sensed a horrible, inescapable . . . not exactly evil — soulless? — destructive force."

The stark simplicity of Jasirey's insight also chilled the council.

She shrugged. "Then the lights came on."

"We are not given a view of our entire future," Master Kai said. "Events not revealed in their entirety may be alterable. Let us dwell on this and seek any available answers through meditation and prayer. Your immediate path requires your full attention."

"One further question, please," a woman said. "Do you remember anything of the ceremony for choosing your husbands?"

"Nothing concrete except a white lion, maybe a metaphor for something, though it wouldn't surprise me if you had a real lion."

Master Kai's eyes crinkled. "Only men shared the Imperiatu with you. Nevertheless, a strong vision. Hold it close."

Jasirey hadn't the energy to decipher that advice.

"Anything else?"

"A guy who didn't want to take part in the husband thing. He needed to leave the island to find his path."

"You gained that knowledge in what way, please?"

"No idea. It happened? Did I do something wrong?"

"No, dear one. Thank you for your patience."

She had in fact delivered closure on Mtombe's hasty departure. For security purposes, only a handful of select pilots were given coordinates to the island's airstrip. The people traveled on island craft flown by island personnel. A few, including Ian who lived off-island, had access. Still, anyone leaving the Devoted and perhaps harboring bitter feelings posed a potential threat. Relieved, the council would mark Mtombe's file status as satisfactory.

Master Kai supported Jasirey's elbow. After sitting, she rose stiffly. The council approached one by one to kiss her cheeks. The tightness in her chest eased. The voices of her approaching men whisked away any remaining tension.

Silly.

Master Kai kissed Jasirey and winked at the men. "Gentlemen, ensure our lady receives the rest she requires."

She looked exhausted. Ian reserved his suggestive comments, allowed the others a hug, and lifted her to head for the cabin. She trailed kisses up and down his neck.

"Behave, woman."

"Uh-huh." She mouthed his ear.

He tossed her to Lee, who deftly caught their flailing wife. "Fellow husbands," Ian said in a sonorous tone, "I have on occasion warned our wife that spanking may be an appropriate option for dealing with a recalcitrant woman."

"I'll whap you back, "she said.

"Good deal," Lee said. "What damage can she inflict?"

"Want me to show you, you big bear?" She pulled his dreadlocks.

Liu took charge. "Nap first, play later. There is a swimming pond we can bring you to if you wish."

The island had a natural harbor for boats and a high, rugged coastline—no beaches.

Jasirey fell asleep before reaching the cabin.

❧ ❧ ❧

"Where are the bathing suits?"

"We don't use them." Lee maintained a straight face as his wife froze mid limp to the wardrobe and crossed her arms, a very cute pout, he thought, flirting about her lips. "I'm teasing, last drawer of the wardrobe."

She accidentally on purpose trod on his foot. "Creep," she added for good measure.

Liu had the group stop at the infirmary first, a bright white building intended to stand out. He removed their lady's dressings, applied a glutinous ointment, and reapplied tighter bandages to protect against possible contaminants from the pond.

The day had warmed a good thirty degrees from the morning's temperature. Jasirey commented on fewer people traveling the paths and was told that many were preparing for the next day's ceremonies. She halted abruptly.

"What ceremonies? I thought I'd finished."

Lee shook his head. "A bunch of dolts, we forgot to tell you." He twirled her about. "We are celebrating finding our Jasirey."

"My husbands aren't dolts." A fond smile erased the prim purse of her lips. After Liu described the joyful welcome of Jasirey and the people's pledge of loyalty and service—the fealty ceremony, Jasirey said, "Whoa. Hope it's everyone at once and not an all-night event."

"They shall greet you by families and affiliations to shorten the process," Fael said.

Ian placed an arm around her waist. "Afterward comes the wedding celebration."

Jasirey stopped again, but Ian's arm propelled her forward.

"Since I'm an American citizen," he said, "you and I will legally marry at home. This one is for the five of us."

Jasirey gave them a wide-eyed look. "Things move awfully fast here. You should have guideposts."

Ian paused atop a hill, the forest's end, to let her take in the postcard scene below: a large dusky blue pond, the back and right side hemmed by a steep tree-lined bank with a thick stand of cattails on the left and skirted in front by a narrow manmade beach. Sand continued several feet into the water to prevent water plants from ensnaring children's legs.

Fael warned that the bottom dropped precipitously past a pebbled berm.

Red-flowered shrubs dotted the hill, and multicolored wildflowers clustered in the grass. Few that day took advantage of a section close to the water mowed for sitting.

Liu suggested swimming to the shaded top right corner to escape the glaring sun.

At the water's edge, Jasirey asked if anything besides plants lived in the pond—anything that had teeth, for instance. Assured nothing poisonous or that bit lived in the pond, she walked in. She expected the water to be cold like the spring-fed lakes at home. The pleasant warmth soothed her aching knees. She swam on her back, making it easier for her hands.

After a while, Lee secured her to his raft of a chest and steered closer to the bank where a flowering tree, its branches naturally drooping, touched the water. He slipped behind its screen of dark pink, tubular flowers dispensing a tangy citrus scent. The pair settled on a ledge protruding from the bank a foot below the surface.

"The perfect make-out spot," Jasirey said. She rested on Lee's lap and traced his beautiful features with soft butterfly kisses. He cupped her head to increase the length and pressure. Small nips of pleasure quivered down her center.

"We thought you might enjoy individual dates. Lucky me, I drew the long straw."

He lowered her bathing suit to lick and suck from neck to breasts. Stronger currents coursed through her. Hanging the suit on a nearby branch, Lee turned her backward, her legs straddling his. It reminded her of the single time she'd ridden a horse. He pulled her toward his erection, his haste unnerving her. He was so huge. Lee nudged her torso lower. She automatically splayed her fingers on his lap for balance and drew in a sharp breath of pain. Lee lifted her at once.

"I'm sorry, little one. I didn't think. Rest your arms on mine. I've got you." He gently lowered her again.

She felt him at her labia, and her hands flailed. "Lee."

"No worries." Keeping her in a secure hold, he eased through her valley.

Ian had shown her this technique. Shame made her eyes sting. "Sorry, Lee."

"You're tired. Relax and let me love you." Lee coaxed his sweet wife beyond thought, glad she couldn't see the hard light in his eyes aimed at those who'd made trust difficult for her.

Hard hot flesh massaging Jasirey's clitoris and the cooler lapping of the water saturated her senses. Without the leverage to press into him, she surrendered her body to Lee. The simple movement produced extraordinary pleasure. Her breathing escalated. He rocked her faster and held her arching body through the orgasm and lingering spasms.

Careful to bank his burning passion in tenderness, Lee turned his wife to face him. Her arms and legs held her body poised above him. His lips molded, his teeth grazed, and a knowing tongue soon had her lowering to join with him. A soft cry against Lee's mouth declared her second climax. Straddling him, she sheathed most of his length.

Her strong thighs gripped him as she searched for the depth she could handle, lifted, and squeezed. Lee caressed her heavy breasts and rounded fanny, his epitome of womanhood.

Jasirey concentrated on the pleasure she saw in his eyes and felt shuddering through him. She forgot her own response but didn't care. Lee did. He grasped her waist and rotated his hips until her eyes glazed in surprised arousal. Sweat trickled between her breasts despite the cool water, and she soon felt nothing save Lee's body winding hers so tightly that her teeth ground together.

Lee's indiscreet release drowned out his wife's sweet, high-pitched cries. Her arms scrambled to hold on. Lee folded her onto his lap and leaned against the bank. *Such a magnificent woman.* Grateful and blessed to be hers, he felt . . . *hell, damned good.*

After granting the pair five minutes, Fael parted the flowery curtain. "You frightened the other swimmers." He grinned at Lee, whose eyes cracked open in a halfhearted glare.

Liu pushed sodden hair from their wife's eyes.

Not quite ready to rejoin the quartet, she snuggled closer to Lee.

"Sorry to interrupt, precious one. I wish to remove you from the water to prevent your body temperature from lowering."

"Killjoy," she said, a contented complaint.

Liu and Fael dressed Jasirey and handed her to Ian, the strongest swimmer. She insisted on leaving the water unassisted and shivered. They'd forgotten towels. Sitting on the grass to dry, the men blocked their wife from the breeze.

"Why'd you come to the island, Ian?" Jasirey asked.

"A recruiter approached me in college. I faced what I considered a bleak future of corporate drudgery in the family business. The mission of the Devoted, to aid troubled areas of the world in preparation for Jasirey, struck me as a worthwhile adventure. Since I still had school, the Devoted agreed to spread my probationary period over the summers.

"The physical training pushed me beyond what I believed possible. The mental training stripped bare my ego and motivation. My true agenda—rebellion against my parents' prescribed future for me. Despite that, the council sent me on missions. We built refugee camps, schools, wells." His brow furrowed. "I heard news stories of disaster victims, saw pictures of poverty-stricken neighborhoods, but in person, the smells of sewage, death, lack of clean water and food, helplessness, and worse, hopelessness, hit harder than a TV screen."

His wife's eyes glowed at Ian. He ran a thumb over her cheek. Her destiny demanded so much more. *Too soon to burden her,* though. Ian heeded Fael's warning glance.

Her gaze became questioning. *Good God, two mind readers.*

He returned to his story.

"I became a member of the Devoted and embarked on a vision quest required of all the Devoted before choosing what we Americans call a career path. It showed me that instead of being a burden, the family corporation could serve as a conduit for Devoted enterprises. My father still held the reins after I graduated, which gave me leeway to join the Protectors and missions. I eventually led some, helped train these three, and commanded them. We work well together."

Jasirey cut to the heart. "You bonded. You're kindred spirits like me and Lizzie, my best friend at home," she said to the others. "Your business—are you happy in it, my Ian?"

"I've added branches that interest and challenge me, human relief organizations I believe make a difference. I've never regretted returning to it."

She hugged him. The men saw clearly that no one had better threaten the welfare of her loved ones. Her stomach rumbled, and Ian pulled her to her feet.

❦ ❦ ❦

A couple waited at the cabin and bowed to Jasirey. The stunning Middle Eastern woman had raven hair in a long braid. "I am Kharia, a cook. My husband agreed to assist in serving dinner."

She leaned in confidentially. "I can handle feeding five people. I think Robin wished a closer view." She giggled.

Jasirey knew she'd met a friend.

After dinner, Fael beside her on the patio swing, Jasirey tugged his silky hair. "Tag, you're it." She laughed at his blank stare. "Sorry, it means time for your story."

He draped an arm over her shoulders. "My memories begin as in immigrant to Iran. A raid on our village in Afghanistan had killed my parents." Jasirey clasped his free hand. She brought Fael a lightness and fullness of heart previously unknown to him. He kept their hands linked.

"My father's brother and his wife assumed my care. They treated me well, yet as I matured, I recognized the burden placed on them. They had three children and inadequate means to support us. A good man gifted in metal work apprenticed me at thirteen. Eventually, he believed I had surpassed the knowledge he possessed. He introduced me to a master who, unknown to him, was also a recruiter. At sixteen, I found my home on the island. Fascinated by Jasirey's legend, I pursued training with single-minded dedication."

A legend's fascination, the island was home. The Devoted's expectations of Jasirey worried her far more than the name she had started to get used to. Despite her misgivings about Fael's revelations, Jasirey allowed only support to show on her face. "How old are you?" she asked.

"You, a living woman, are of far greater importance than a legend. I love and want you. Age does not signify."

"Means you're not much older than Liu."

"The Imperiat hoped you'd accept at least two in their twenties," Lee said.

"Right, playmates for my kids." She smiled at the men's laughter and prompted Fael. "You were fascinated."

He brought her hand to his lips. "The Imperiat refused me as a Protector. They felt I lacked balance, the will or ability to form relationships, so I refocused on metal work, discovered an affinity for farming, and studied psychology. I learned that my uncontrolled empathic abilities left me open to others' feelings. In self-protection, I kept my distance from people. I trained to block them." Fael sensed that his aversion to a gift organic to how she herself interacted with others puzzled her.

"Ian, Lee, and Liu relied on me, taught me how to relate to other people. I underwent the vision quest, and the Imperiat approved my induction into the Protectors of Jasirey." Fael cradled his wife's face. "We found you, a real woman with normal flaws and fears and exceptional gifts, empathic as am I. You also possess an innate compassionate tolerance I merely aspire to, a capacity to love that amazes me. I adore you, most beloved."

Tears pooled in Jasirey's eyes. She climbed onto Fael's lap to whisper in his ear. "Whose turn is it tonight?" She wriggled in invitation over his immediate reaction.

Taking pity on Fael's near panic, Liu recommended he flirt back. He, Lee, and Ian walked off to discuss their friend's illuminating insights.

Despite his words, Fael idolized Jasirey. Being chosen by her at times felt like a dream. Simply being near her could drive him to the edge of his control. Fearing embarrassing himself, he breathed to regain his composure, removed their clothes, and skin-to-skin, pleasured his wife's sensitive spots. She had many.

"I wish I could touch you the way I want to," she said.

Her smile filled Fael's heart. She touched him profoundly. He knelt, draped her legs over his shoulders, and with a wicked grin lowered his long mobile tongue. Her body bowed, and her fingers gripped the swing. Fael quickly propelled her into an explosive climax. Eyes glittering in the semidarkness, he locked her legs about his waist, drew the swing toward him, and buried himself in his wife's tight caress.

Jasirey's muted sex noises inflamed Fael. He varied his tempo and depth, not letting her find a rhythm. She mewled, her strong body lifting, seeking. He held the peak until his body took control. Together, they ignited in kaleidoscopic flares and sparks. Fael gasped for air but managed to heave their bodies across the swing. He rested his head on Jasirey's breast and caressed her damp pubic curls.

Jasirey never had shaved, and none of her men found it weird. She might love them for that alone. The moon rose. She studied the sculpted musculature of her viper with frank curiosity and doubted he had an ounce of extra padding. "Tell me more about your life."

"As my lady wishes." Fael smiled as she giggled, a lovely, contented sound. "We lived among other Afghanis, survival our primary concern, which meant rarely becoming involved in the political or religious strife rampant in Iran. I had little awareness of world events or other cultures till gaining access to education here. I . . . " He searched for an appropriate simile. "A parched sponge, I gratefully absorbed every drop." Fael regarded Jasirey. "I know little about you, either. I am a Muslim. Are you a religious person?"

"Depends on what you mean by religious. I'm Christian, more liberal than fundamental. I was a Sunday school teacher when my kids were young."

Jasirey gazed up at the moon, and Fael thought she would say no more.

"Many Christians believe the Bible was written by God's authority, like Muslims and the Quran, I suppose."

"I am thinking you do not."

"It's an important learning tool, but I think the point of Jesus's story was our forgiveness, receiving the Holy Spirit to guide and teach us. I love reading the Bible but find too many discrepancies to take it literally. My faith relies on God's Spirit."

Jasirey gave Fael a sober smile and continued. "I wonder if you'll like living in America. US law separates government from religion, and society has become either overly separated or authoritarian in pronouncing rules. Bugs some Christians who denounce the government for being too big, too interfering, then complain when towns don't put up Christmas decorations or promote prayer in schools. Which prayers, I'd like to know. Should the kids bring prayer rugs, rosary beads, a mantra?" Jasirey shrugged. "Not an issue in Muslim religion?"

"Muslims are the people who practice the religion of Islam, which means surrender or submission to the will of Allah. Interpretations of Sharia, the moral code and religious laws, obviously differ, sometimes to the point of violent confrontations, though practicing Muslims agree that the Quran is Allah's eternal and infallible word, revealed to His prophet Muhammad."

Fael smiled ruefully. "I sound pedantic. We respect one another's beliefs here, but all agree on our service to Jasirey. I have not thought through how different ideas and practices might clash, as you say they do in America, without such a unifying force."

"Understandable. Dogmatic people think that holding fast to their doctrines requires zero tolerance for other beliefs. I find such rigidity more an armor against fear. Like a house of cards, even the smallest doubt or question about the belief structure will send it all crashing down—fear, not true faith. But enough of my rambling. Please continue, I don't find you pedantic. I know little about Islam. Different cultures and religions fascinate me."

Fael kissed her. "Which is why you are Jasirey. But as you wish. Muslims follow the Five Pillars—the confession of faith: there is one God and Muhammad is his prophet, prayer, charity, fasting, and pilgrimage. One day I shall describe to you my pilgrimage to Mecca, the hajj. The faithful are called to undertake the journey at least once in their lifetime. People journey from all over the world to worship in fellowship."

The moon rose higher, and Fael brought their most precious lady to bed. Once she slept, he washed, unrolled his prayer rug, set its head toward Mecca, and performed the end-of-day ritualistic prayer of the Salat. Finished, he turned to prayerful supplication for their family and for Jasirey in her journey to comprehend a destiny that would encompass many religions and cultures.

The Leap Forward

The celebration day dawned hot and hazy with showers forecasted for the afternoon. The people considered rain, a clichéd but venerated symbol of growth and renewal, a blessing on the fealty and marriage ceremony. The husbands hurriedly kissed their wife and ran off to finish business for the festivities.

Jasirey looked forward to the wedding and dreaded the fealty ceremony. The people believed her to be someone significant when she'd done nothing to earn such status. Her injuries even precluded helping with the preparations.

Inactivity worsened her mood, so Jasirey paced. Trees filtered the sun. Nonetheless, exercise left her sticky and irritable. Sitting on the edge of the bed, she practiced a calming exercise, once and then a second time for good measure. Legs dangling over the edge, she lay back. *What if the people found her a disappointment?*

She woke as Liu lifted her legs. "Not the best position for sleeping," he said.

Her eyes misted, and she diverted her gaze.

"Precious one, please do not hide your feelings."

The caring tore at her control. Tears spurted and Jasirey attempted to curl away.

Liu lifted her upright to rub her back. "Tell me what troubles you."

"I haven't done anything to deserve this attention. It's awkward."

"Our gifts signify our pledge of fealty, our responsibilities to you."

"I don't understand."

"Do not underestimate your gift to us."

"That's the problem. What have I given the people other than a promise?"

"You embody our dreams for a more secure world. It is not a small sacrifice we ask. You alter your life for no reason other than our faith in you."

"When has the world ever experienced global harmony?"

"Even a small ripple can travel throughout the pond."

She gave him a wan smile. "For me, being Jasirey means you, Fael, Lee, and Ian. You're my reality. I promise to do my best, be your figurehead, but few can live up to such high hopes. Human symbols have flaws, tend to disappoint. What then?"

Liu appreciated humility and had no wish to overwhelm her. She lacked insight into her powers. Even the Imperiat had not yet determined their extent. "Master Kai asks you to join him for lunch." A greater counselor did not exist.

Jasirey brightened. *Weird. She barely knew the man.* "I've been wondering what the Protectors will do now. I'll ask him."

"In regard to?"

"I've chosen my husbands. There's no point in them continuing to wait."

That had not occurred to Liu. "I shall be interested in the answer." He escorted his wife to the Imperiat domicile and questioned her on her family's prayer traditions.

"Roger felt self-conscious praying aloud," she said. "I prayed with the kids until they wanted to say their own."

Liu suspected this spiritual gap contributed to the dissolution of their marriage.

"For myself," she continued, "I pray as the need or whim strikes. Do you practice a particular religion? I know the Communist party is officially atheist."

"Yes. Chinese people, however, especially since the party has softened on religious practice, seldom profess atheism. Chinese religion is practical, the good of family and society in the here and now considered sacred rather than the pursuit of a deity. Confucianism, still ingrained in Chinese society, though perhaps more a philosophy than a religion, concentrates on human relationships rather than on immortality or salvation. Inferiors owe superiors obedience—subject to official, wife to husband, child to parent, younger to elder sibling. The only equal relationship is friend to friend. Of course," he continued, "one-child policies, the migration of people from rural to urban areas, and the changes in women's independence influence these beliefs."

Jasirey said, "I've read that, despite improving rights for women, female landowners have been attacked, even killed, to prevent the property from leaving the male's family, and some women have been kidnapped and forced to marry in remote areas."

"A serious issue, but one for another time." Liu could not help reacting to his precious one's sparking eyes. "Had you rejected me, I might have resorted to such crude methods."

"Shut up."

Liu grinned. "In the old traditions, men cared for elderly parents and continued the family line while daughters became part of the family they married into. The preference for sons continues today, and males outnumber females, though rewriting one-child policies may alter that in time."

"Trying to mold nature or societies into a political image seldom works well. Anyway, in America the saying goes: a daughter is yours for the rest of her life, a son, until he marries a wife. But there is something else I read about. Feng shui is trendy for setting up homes in America. Is it a religion?"

"Also more of a philosophy once outlawed by the party, intended to ensure harmony among the invisible forces called Qi that bind people, the universe, and the earth together, energies expressed by yin and yang. Yang creates a force and yin receives it, their polar natures providing a system of checks and balances between harmony and conflict or diversity and unity. Although opposite, the properties of relationships such as light-dark, high-low, hot-cold, life-death define both."

"A philosophy that would come in handy as Jasirey. And your personal beliefs?"

"On the island, I came to believe in a higher power who offers guidance in our earthly tasks. The people pray together, whatever our beliefs. I believe in the power of prayer. There is something called noetic science that explores how beliefs, thoughts, and intentions affect the physical world, psychic abilities, and how the mind might affect bodily health. I believe prayer and meditation are such devices."

"I'd like to research the science," Jasirey said. "It wouldn't surprise me if the Devoted as a whole could do that."

Liu took the observation seriously. "With you at the helm, most certainly."

The couple had kept to the shade. Even so, Jasirey wiped her face every few yards, her lungs resisting the heavy air. The sheltering trees eventually opened to a Zen garden with a small Buddha perched atop stones in one corner. Artistic patterns raked into a square of sand intrigued her, but the sun's glare off its white starkness stabbed into her eyes.

Liu steered her to the domicile built inside a tree-topped hill and fronted in tinted glass. He tapped a hanging bell and, after a gentle kiss, relinquished his wife to a man who ushered her to Master Kai.

He waited next to a low table set for two in a sparsely furnished room. A skylight bathed muted sunshine over an entire wall of ivy and ferns hung in growth-medium pockets.

Jasirey admired the use of space.

Master Kai regarded Jasirey's damp face. Knowing she would politely dismiss his concern, he poured glasses of her preferred cold tea. "Shall we eat now or wait till you have rested?"

"I'm afraid the heat's taken away my appetite. Please, suit yourself." The pain brewing above her eyes abated in the room's coolness.

"We shall wait. I asked you here to voice any objections, questions, or concerns relating to tonight. Your choice of husbands pleases you?"

A soft rose tinged her pale face. "Yes, I love them. It's weird." Master Kai's lips twitched, and she said, "You have to admit we stray from the norm."

"You are not the average family. This troubles you?"

"Sure. My husbands are used to the Devoted's complete acceptance. I'd hate for them to be unhappy at home."

"Be at ease. Your husbands' training included skills for adapting."

Jasirey pushed her glass around its small pool of condensation. "Faith seems to be an integral part of being a member of the Devoted. I believe we're created in God's image, creative and with an infinite capacity to love, but I wonder if you have any atheists or agnostics."

"As you say, faith in your destiny is of paramount importance to the Devoted. Anyone unwilling to accede to this would not be accepted. Nonetheless, we do have people of both beliefs who accept your destiny even if they do not believe in a deity. Now, dear one, what else weighs on you?"

Jasirey shrugged. "If some guy asked me to become his second, third, or fourth wife, I'd tell him to go to hell. What if one of my husbands decides the same?"

"Training accustomed your husbands long ago to the realities of a relationship with Jasirey."

"Ian didn't train as a Protector, though."

"He began the training and has worked closely with Lee, Liu, and Fael, who completed it. He understands what is required. They all tell me you do not wish to be released from them, nor do they wish to be released from you. They did, however, express concern that it may be some time before you accept yourself as Jasirey."

"It's awkward. The people treat me as though I've already earned the title."

"The fealty ceremony may provide what you seek."

When he didn't elaborate, she said, "Which is?"

He pressed a hand over hers. "Open your heart to the people, and they will be satisfied. Enjoy tonight. Let that suffice for the present."

Jasirey considered hugging him. Afraid it was too familiar, she refrained.

Master Kai read her expressive face and comfortably embraced her.

❧ ❧ ❧

The family decided on a pre-ceremony nap. Jasirey woke with a raging headache. She rose quietly. Her men lay apart to prevent their body heat from disrupting her rest. Knowing the bathroom lacked a medicine cabinet, she held a cold cloth to her forehead and searched the wardrobe for her purse. She had a bottle of ibuprofen tucked in a pocket.

"You okay, baby?" Ian asked.

Jasirey jumped. *The man was quiet on his feet.* "Looking for my purse."

Coming up behind Ian, Liu noted pain-pinched lines between their wife's eyes, fetched his bag, and placed a thermometer in her ear.

"I'm not sick," Jasirey said. "Just a headache from the humidity. Ibuprofen takes care of it."

"I wish to rule out heat stroke. Temperature normal. I prefer not to resort to drugs. May I use acupuncture to relieve the pain?"

The needle part didn't bother Jasirey. They supposedly didn't hurt. On the bed, she closed her eyes. Liu's hands deftly touched here and there. The headache dissipated faster than if she'd taken pills. Lee and Fael each clasped a foot to massage.

"You guys have good hands," she said. "If we're ever strapped for cash, we can hire you out." She peered at her men and appreciated the view.

Liu recommended a cool shower and drying off beneath the sitting area fan. After, Ian lifted a garment bag from the wardrobe and withdrew a gown that shimmered in the muted colors of the ring the Imperiatu had given her. It had cap sleeves and an empire waist, fit snugly at the bodice, and flowed to the ankle. The material settled about her curves, the skirt opening at one leg to mid thigh.

Her men's eyes glittered in appreciation, and she admired their sleeveless wrap shirts that tied to the side and showed off fit arms and chests. Ian wore dark brown, hunter green for Lee, Liu in plum, and Fael in cobalt blue.

An honor guard waited outside to escort Jasirey. Six Protectors, eyes glued to their radiant lady, bowed. A padded armchair sat on a platform attached to two long poles.

"Seriously?" she whispered.

Liu elbowed her.

Noting the gravity of the bearers' demeanor, she stifled a giggle.

One of the bearers settled her on the chair's cushion while Ian and Liu lit torches and stood at the front, Lee and Fael behind. The six bearers crouched to grasp the poles.

Jasirey grabbed hold of the chair's arms but experienced nary a bobble as the platform rose to the Protectors' shoulders. From her perch, she enjoyed the soft turquoise sky festively garlanded by dark coral clouds streaked with royal purple. In the forest, water beads from the afternoon shower clung to leaves and gleamed in the torchlight. Jasirey loved the earthy, after-a-rain scent. A cacophony of conversation swelled over her and hushed when a horn heralded the group's entry into a large meadow. In harmony, the people bowed together, a plain of upturned faces undulating like grass in the wind.

The Protectors stopped at a raised platform. The council stood behind a chair placed in the middle. They saluted Jasirey. The bearers lowered the conveyance and helped her onto the platform as the husbands moved aside.

Master Kai offered his arm and turned their lady to face the crowd. Iridescent in the setting sun, she gave them her shy smile. The people gazed, awestruck, and erupted into a frenzy of cheers.

Her small fingers tensed on Master Kai's arm. He permitted the outpouring to continue until her shoulders relaxed and laughter bubbled from her animated face. He raised his hand for quiet. "We gather to pledge fealty to Jasirey, our most precious lady. Any wishing not to vow allegiance, withdraw now."

Jasirey's eyes widened. No one moved. Master Kai seated her with courtly elegance.

The council kneeled together, and a councilwoman said, "We pledge our fealty. We live to serve Jasirey." She presented a hand-carved wooden bowl in polished tiger-eye colors and said, "We give you our vow that you and yours shall never go hungry."

Sentiment softened Jasirey's thanks to a whisper.

The Imperiat and Elders followed, pledged their fealty, and handed her a deep-purple, hand-blown pitcher with a fluted spout. "We give you our vow that you and yours shall never go thirsty."

A delegation from the Protectors of Jasirey knelt. She searched their faces for disgruntlement but saw only devotion.

The Protectors had chosen Kimika to present their gift, an alabaster fertility figure.

A synaptic charge of deep recognition surged through Jasirey. "My white lion."

Kimika trembled as he handed the statue to their lady. "To watch over you in pregnancy and labor. I am Kimika."

Jasirey wanted to give the sweet, bumbling young man—all of them, really—something in return. "I appreciate your dedication to Jasi—to me. You weren't chosen, and I'll be honest, I don't see it, but the council believes some of you may still become fathers of . . . my children." Hope blazed on their faces. Her eyes returned to Kimika. "Not you." She blushed. "Don't be offended. You feel like one of my sons."

Kimika launched forward, stopped short of touching their lady, and bowed.

Murmuring in excited whispers, the Protectors backed away. Jasirey hoped she'd done the right thing. She hadn't yet discussed the Protectors' status with Kai.

Fael rejoiced as he sensed a subtle, proprietary shift in their wife's feelings toward the people. He and the other husbands often felt a surge of strength and well-being in her presence. Judging from their adoring smiles, the people felt a semblance of the same. Fael recognized the toll that blocking his empathic abilities exacted on his strength and wondered what it cost her to refrain from her natural predilection to project her emotions onto others.

Barraged by families and work-related groups, Jasirey delighted in their thoughtful gifts, mostly products of the island—honey, flower and vegetable seeds, hand-dyed yarn. They'd been informed of her hobbies.

Lee's father, Paul, mother, Alva, and sister Beryl and her family stepped onto the platform. Welcoming them as family, Jasirey kissed their cheeks. "We'll set a time to get together," she said.

Lee's family bowed, happy with his and their good fortune.

When only the husbands remained to give their pledges, Ian stepped forward and placed an engagement ring on Jasirey's finger. "I pledge loyalty, service, and my heart. This ring has been in my family for generations." His knee met the floor. "Marry me, my love. This is the formal proposal."

Jasirey's arms circled his neck as she joined her mouth to his. The people hooted and cheered.

Lee followed and presented a wood carving of the pond and the flowering tree, each flower distinct, trailing into the rippling water. "You make my life complete. I am yours always."

"Lee, it's wonderful." On tiptoe, she thanked him, kissing him several times.

Liu offered a wooden box containing lined drawers filled with loose-leaf teas and inscribed with Chinese characters. "Calligraphy, a small talent from your playful ferret. I love you, precious one. I am yours always."

She pulled his head to hers and, unmindful of the audience, gently bit his lower lip.

The people loved Jasirey's sometimes edgy but always good-hearted impishness.

Fael's eyes glowed lava gold. "Beloved, I pledge my fealty. I am and shall ever be yours." He handed her a metal sculpture of a log around which ranged an eagle, a bear, a ferret, and a snake, the eyes bearing a marked resemblance to the man represented.

"I'll treasure this always." She twined her fingers into his mink soft hair. Their bodies fit together for a tender kiss.

Master Kai returned to Jasirey's side. "We, the Devoted, have pledged our loyalty and service. Do you, Shannon, vow forevermore to be Jasirey and accept us as your people?"

"I do."

The people saluted and bowed. She reciprocated, which surprised no one. Word spread rapidly regarding Jasirey's every word and deed, always the prime topic of conversation.

Jasirey looked out at the sea of loving and hopeful faces. Figuring out their expectations, let alone meeting them, would daunt even the most stout-hearted. She also had to decipher the images from her prophecy, the key to understanding her destiny.

Jasirey took a deep breath, breathed out, and released her worries and concerns. She first needed to concentrate on becoming a family as she and her men wed in the Devoted tradition. For the moment, she would take Master Kai's suggestion and let her new husbands' and the people's loving acceptance be enough.

❧ ❧ ❧

Jasirey woke with her dream playing in her head. On the forest path to their honeymoon cabin, she watched as—wrists bound together by a billowing white silk ribbon—she and Ian, Lee, Liu, and Fael pivoted, swung, and stepped together. The ribbon binding the dancers and the torch they carried arced about them in white and gold in beautiful celebration.

When fully awake, Jasirey kissed her sleepy men ranging like sun rays about her. She hated to disturb them, but nature called. Five people and one bathroom in the small cottage got tricky. Earning mega points, the men insisted she use it first. She'd have been okay leaving the toilet seat up, since the men outnumbered the woman. They always lowered it. If they ever missed, she never had to clean it up.

They needed to talk. She had not planned to be gone so long from her sons. The Devoted did not expect her to live on their home island, but the paperwork to have Liu, Fael, and Lee join them in America would take time.

Should she bring it up, discuss the dynamics of their new marriage and becoming a family with Christopher and Michael? It was, after all, their honeymoon and maybe not the ideal time to make decisions and plans.

The newlyweds ate breakfast on the patio where Liu asked her for a dinner date.

"I'd like that. Later, when the time difference works out, I'll call my kids. I need an idea of how long we'll be gone. I don't want to burden Everett."

"We discussed that," Lee said. "Might you agree to bring them to the island?"

"The people look forward to meeting your sons," Fael said. "The Devoted's acceptance of our family might facilitate the boys' acceptance of you as Jasirey, us as your husbands, and themselves as Jasirey's children."

"They're regular kids. I won't burden them with adult expectations."

"No, precious one, of course not," Liu said. "Training classes are underway to teach the people to answer your children's questions in an age-appropriate manner."

Cool, but . . . "Kids process a lot of influences." Her ex, Roger, had entrenched prejudices, and the small western Massachusetts town where they lived lacked diversity.

"Don't worry, love," Ian said. "Bringing the boys here may iron out many difficulties. If you agree, we prefer to stay until the house is finished and the legalities finalized for Lee, Liu, and Fael."

"This is a lovely place for a honeymoon," Fael said.

Jasirey had no argument for that. "But doesn't a house take months to build? Roger won't appreciate having his sons gone that long."

"Our crew shall consist of Devoted builders, plumbers, and electricians dedicated to one project versus the average construction company's multiple, simultaneous projects."

"For our privacy and the boys' comfort," Liu said, "Robin and Kharia have offered their home to them. They live not far from this cabin and have sons your boys' ages."

Fael sensed her uncertainty. "This provides time to become accustomed to us at their pace and a sounding board in ready-made friends. We suggest contact via computer before their arrival to ease the introduction."

Debating whether to be touched or annoyed, Jasirey said, "That was a lot of thinking."

Lee smiled. "Always with the intention of talking to you about it. They're your kids."

Ian kissed her forehead. "I have business in Boston next week. Shall I bring the boys back with me?"

Jasirey saw no better option and burrowed into Ian. What was she doing to her babies?

❧ ❧ ❧

After lunch, the men left to attend to business before a meeting scheduled with the Imperiat.

Jasirey tried napping. Unsettled, she chose a daffodil yellow dress, grabbed the bag of yarn and a hook she'd received at the fealty ceremony, and went outside to the porch swing.

Grateful for the help of Master Kai, she wanted to make him an afghan either for decoration or for occasional cooler nights she was told descended on the island in the dry season. A simple design in Jasirey's colors stuck in her mind—a blue sky, green meadow with a blue stream and wildflowers, and one lone purple flower in the middle.

When her hands tired from crocheting, Jasirey walked to the marketplace to pick up ingredients for dinner. People shopping there helped her plan a meal easy to make despite the wounds on her hands.

Master Kai joined them, and Jasirey smiled in greeting. "Kai, just the person I want to talk to." The people stilled. *Oh, dear.* Embarrassed, she appealed to him. "I meant no offense. Master doesn't pop into my head when I see you." She winced at the probable second faux pas.

"Nor should you." Master Kai dismissed the nonexistent gaffe. "For you have always been my master." He smiled at the people's astonishment and Jasirey's puzzlement. He asked for glasses of cold tea and carried them to a shaded table.

The people understood Master Kai would have sent them away if they weren't welcome. They settled on the ground, which further perplexed Jasirey.

"My life has entwined with yours throughout the centuries. One earthly treasure binds me to this plane—you." He smiled at Jasirey's stunned look. "I have loved you and been your dearest friend, at times your husband. A woman of light and love, fated to be Jasirey, you decided to explore the darker side of humanity in preparation. Cruelty, abuse, neglect—you suffered them on your own to experience loneliness. I knew, when you were ready to become Jasirey, destiny would bring us together again."

Trying to process, Jasirey understood at least one thing. Kai had suffered loneliness on account of her. *Did one apologize for choices made in some unremembered life?*

Master Kai signaled the people. They rose, bowed reverently, and departed. Before nightfall, everyone on the island would hear of the encounter in the marketplace. Master Kai pushed Jasirey's drink closer. She drank two-thirds in one draft.

"Saying I did experience the things you mentioned, not sure what I learned other than a compulsion to control, a horrible trait."

Master Kai frowned at her scoffing tone. "The wish to control generally revolves around benefiting oneself. That does not describe you."

"I learned to repress it after an incident with a friend who used to sing with me. I heard of an open mike contest but was too cowardly to go alone. Even shyer than I was, she said no. I kept harping at her, refusing to take no for an answer. When I arrived to pick her up, she had fled her own home to get away from me. I was mad till the bullying ugliness of what I'd done sank in. I apologized, surprised she agreed to talk to me, but the friendship dissolved soon after."

Master Kai cradled her hands. "It requires many lifetimes to master the darker forces of our nature. I am certain you have labored to understand and overcome them. Without flaws, dearest one, could you then understand and forgive the fallibility of others?" Tears sprang into her troubled eyes. "You said you wished to speak to me."

Jasirey gazed at him blankly, then blinked to clear her vision. "Right. My head's whirling."

"Best to think on it later after you have rested."

He had such caring eyes. "Kai . . . may I call you Kai?"

"As it pleases you."

"Have you ever been my father?"

An unexpected question. "I have not. The idea gives me much to contemplate. First, however, your question. I must soon depart to meet your husbands."

"Oh, right. I wondered what happens to the Protectors now that I'm married. I hope they won't remain devoted to me and unmarried. That wouldn't be fair."

"Agreed. The Imperiat shall discuss this, speak to the Protectors, and apprise you of the outcome." Master Kai warmly embraced her.

Jasirey felt acceptance and comfort from Kai, though the husband-and-wife part threw her. She definitely thought of him as a father figure. She wanted to say she loved him but feared aggravating an unrequited love.

He bowed and whispered in her ear. "I love you as well, dearest one." Her flashing grin tunneled into his heart. He had missed her.

❧ ❧ ❧

Ian, Liu, Fael, and Lee met at the Imperiat domicile and were ushered to a room adequate for groups to convene with the Imperiat. The Imperiat served the customary tea.

"Gentlemen," asked a woman, "our most precious lady fares well?"

"Her wounds heal as expected," Liu said, "though she tires easily."

Too early to diagnose pregnancy, that didn't lessen the anticipation. "We have grave concerns relating to Jasirey's prophecy, especially the ordeal she describes after the quadruplet's birth. Historically speaking, four husbands seem inadequate for the task."

Despite the woman's supportive tone, the men's egos bruised.

"Remain aware of your own and each other's energy levels. You need never cope alone. We, your people, are always your support and counsel."

The men bowed in gratitude.

Jasirey saw clearly, Master Kai observed. Her husbands lacked the life experience for facing what lay ahead. Signs suggested greater difficulty than she with all her gifts foresaw. He broached the next subject in especial sympathy for Ian.

"It is critical the children represent our diverse world. We questioned Jasirey and agree the vision decrees the second pregnancy shall be fathered by others, perhaps including someone Jasirey saw as a wild boar."

Ian managed to keep his expression benign. "Does that mean another husband?"

"That, we cannot know."

A man said, "Jasirey's primary concern seems to be whether you can accept the dictates of prophecy. Your resolution to support your wife determines her ability to meet her destiny."

"Physical and emotional bonds between lovers and partners," Master Kai said, "often determine their ability to meet life's challenges. This trait more than doubles with Jasirey and those she chooses to love. Physical and emotional closeness become not only a need but an imperative. Neither side will function well without the other. We believe this phenomenon originates with Jasirey to help her cope with the strenuous demands she must meet to ensure her destiny. Her health, her very existence, shall depend on that bond."

But no pressure. Ian felt a prick at his conscience in remembering his wife saying the same thing to him about she alone having to choose whether to become Jasirey. He realized that acceptance of her destiny would come even harder for her and determined to do his part in aiding her.

When outside and despite their training, rocked by Master Kai's words, the men linked hands to pray.

Afterward, Lee said, "I had no clue Jasirey's vision weighed on her."

Ian sighed. "I warned you she's conditioned to hiding her feelings."

"Yes," Liu said, "I believe she has yet to fully confide her fears of the challenges we face in becoming a family."

Fael pondered. "Perhaps she has reason not to rely on us. Training provides a base to proceed from. None of us possesses the wisdom of experience to offer as a husband or a father."

"Our actions prove our words," Lee said. "Your advice, Ian."

Ian flung an arm around Fael's neck. "I worked alongside you all these years. How did I miss seeing this insightful man?"

They all knew he hadn't missed a thing.

"Is Jasirey our only concern?" Liu asked. "Ian, you followed the path meant for you, business rather than a Protector. Bringing her to the island, you had reservations that eased when she chose us, your friends, as her husbands. I believe the idea of our wife selecting other men upsets you."

Ian rubbed the back of his neck. "I won't deny it."

"Understand that it is acceptable, practically required of her to take lovers. She does so for far more important reasons than mere physical gratification. Our support is vital to her emotional well-being."

"She has the power to better hearts and minds," Fael said, "but no doubt senses your unease, Ian, and fears hurting you."

"Another reason for not telling us the full prophecy. I'll talk to her."

❧ ❧ ❧

Jasirey had been so distracted by Kai's revelations, she'd forgotten to pick up supplies for dinner, which sucked. She pulled herself up from her nap and searched the refrigerator—a bowl of cooked rice, leftover fish, and vegetables. She hoped Liu liked thrown-together concoctions. She arranged an intimate setting on the coffee table in the sitting area, then went to search for a pan in the kitchenette's island cabinet.

Liu entered the cabin quietly in case Jasirey slept. A lovely derrière pointed toward him. He snaked an arm about her and drew her into his instant response. "I shall provide dessert," he murmured. "What do you prepare for dinner?"

Jasirey laughed breathlessly. "Dessert first can be fun."

The healer warred against the libidinous male. He lifted her and, cupping her enticing ass in both hands, devoured Jasirey's lips. He pushed the shoulders of her dress to her elbows, lowered his mouth to a breast, and nibbled inward to its peak with exquisite control. Head flung back, she offered herself and soon arched in climax. Liu held her as she calmed.

"Did you guys train at that?" He merely offered a sexy smile. "Bet you all earned As."

Liu laughed and raised the dress back in place. "Consider that your dessert sample."

Jasirey ran her hand over his bulging pants. "Sure?"

He kissed the tip of her nose. "Behave. I do not wish to rush."

"Uh-huh, you just want me to eat."

"And so you shall." Liu heated the rice mixture, stirred to prevent burning, and brought a steaming bowl to the low table. They sat side by side on cushions. "Similar to fried rice," Liu said. "Very good."

"I'm glad you like it. What did the Imperiat want?"

"To remind us to rely on them as a resource and to inform us we will not father your second pregnancy."

Jasirey's mouth opened, closed. "Why . . . what did Ian say?"

"Your husbands," he said with gentle emphasis, "wonder why you hid this from us."

Jasirey pushed her plate away. "If anything, I hid a bunch of jumbled images. The Imperiat interpreted them—wrongly. I'm too old for one pregnancy, let alone two. I don't want other men."

Liu's brow knit at her vehemence.

"I'm sorry. Weird day, things flying at me left and right. I can't get my bearings."

"To what do you refer? We endeavor to maintain realistic expectations. Trust is earned. You have known three of us for five days—Ian, not much longer."

"Trust is a two-way street. You barely know me either."

"You are Jasirey."

She sighed. "One thing I'm sure of, my Liu. You are the sweetest man."

He toppled her onto the cushions and slanted his mouth over hers, his hands everywhere. Jasirey had no recollection of how she became naked. His mouth raised both goose bumps and a languorous heat that numbed her mind to everything except the pleasure and the love he wished to convey. Lips, tongue, and fingers massaged and prodded her core to a delicious release.

Having held back all evening, Liu felt anything but sweet. Blood firing, he swept the dishes off the table, flung a cushion onto it, and pushed Jasirey facedown over it. Her bubbling laughter burst on a surprised whoosh of air as he gripped her hips and entered in one hard surge.

Jasirey held the table edge for a much different ride. She absorbed each deep penetration until bolts of pleasure sizzled through her, leaving her limbs feeling as though saturated in molten syrup. Jasirey dimly felt Liu's shudders. Seconds? Minutes? Maybe years later, with a ragged laugh, she reached behind her to pat his bottom. "One for the record book."

"Precious one." Liu nuzzled her neck. "Was I too rough?"

"If you hurt me, you'll be sprawled on your excellent butt. Trust me."

"I believe you." He moved them both to the floor cushions so they faced each other. He thrummed fingers up and down her spine.

Jasirey thought that Liu's bone structure had a finer delicacy to it than the others, though she discerned no difference in strength. She tickled his butt cheeks. Liu opened bleary eyes. It sometimes confounded Jasirey how great sex one time sent you sprawling, bottomed out, and another time left you invigorated.

She propped up on Liu's chest. "Want to go skinny-dipping?" His eyes cleared a bit. "No, I see you don't. Stay here. I'll clean up." She kissed him and rose to retrieve her dress. The dishes had survived their abrupt meeting with the floor.

The others returned as Liu zipped his pants. Their eyes brimmed with a blend of amusement and amazement, and Jasirey realized they'd heard of her visit to the marketplace.

"Hi," she said shyly.

"Is something wrong?" Liu asked.

Jasirey brushed crumbs from her dress. "I talked to Kai this afternoon."

"Master Kai."

Lee's grin held a glint of pride. "Not to our wife."

She went still. "I'm going for a walk. You guys fill Liu in."

Ian linked hands. "You've had quite a week, haven't you, baby?" He squeezed her hand as a small forlorn sound caught in her throat. "Stay and talk to us."

"She requires time," Fael said. "No harm can come to her."

Ian trusted his friend's judgment and released her.

Jasirey stepped out into the moonlight, no flashlight necessary. She headed for a flower garden she'd seen on previous walks. The exercise steadied her. Nearing the garden's stone fountain, she saw flowing shadows highlighted in silver. A sweet citrusy scent diffused in a caressing breeze. The soft rush of the fountain soothed her, yet tears plopped onto her chest. Her dress had no pockets, no concealed tissues. She sniffed loudly. A white handkerchief emerged from the shadows and frightened a squeak out of her.

"Forgive me, precious lady. I didn't notice you arrive and then you seemed . . . please." Sitting on a bench, Kimika fluttered the handkerchief.

"Thanks." She used it and sat beside him. "Wrestling with heavy thoughts, too?"

Kimika rose. "You wish to be alone."

"Thought I did. Do you mind staying? Talk awhile?"

Red mottled Kimika's pale cheeks. She looked at him expectantly. He searched for words, blurted out feelings. "Lady, I'm not a lion. I'll disappoint you."

A giggle escaped Jasirey. "Sorry." A full out laugh followed.

Kimika's flash of hurt feelings fizzled at her smile. Warmth cradled him.

"Want to know why I'm out here?" she asked.

He nodded.

"Fear of disappointing all of you, botching the job of being Jasirey."

"But why? You are . . . " He lifted his hands and shoulders. " . . . Jasirey."

"And you're my white lion. Just titles—I don't know what either means. We're jumping into the deep end and hoping we don't drown."

"You seem an excellent swimmer." A grin replaced his hangdog demeanor.

"Geesh, smart asses. I'm always surrounded by smart asses."

Kimika drew a cleansing breath. "It's easier for me, I think—training, people eager to teach me. What will sustain you?"

Loving eyes and supportive hands flashed to mind. "My husbands." Everything she needed waited in the cabin. "The people, you, Master Kai."

"No question."

She glanced at him shyly. "I haven't given much thought as to why I see a white lion."

"The male lion protects the pride—Protector—and I am pale. My father was a blond South African; my mother, Thai."

"They live here?"

"They died in a car accident in South Africa when I was six, the first time my father brought my mother to meet his family. Confronting one hurdle at a time, they left me behind in the care of my grandparents in Thailand."

"Your grandparents raised you?"

"No, their eldest son brought me to his rice farm. Some of my first memories are of standing thigh deep in water, pushing little plants into the mud, and of people throwing water at a cat—a fertility rite. I never learned why." The ruddiness returned to his cheeks. "Anyway, maybe two years later, I boarded a plane for South Africa and my father's sister. Unable to afford mechanical harvesters and such, my uncle lost his farm. The plane—so large it seemed impossible for it to stay in the air."

"They sent you by yourself?"

Flattered by Jasirey's concern, Kimika grinned at the fire in her eyes. "The aunt I came to know would not have paid for an unnecessary person. I was no stranger to frugality. Harder, my aunt insisted I speak Afrikaans or English and go to Catholic school. I was Buddhist. Statues of the suffering Christ came alive in my dreams, though I liked the Madonna holding her child." One corner of his mouth crooked up. "Nuns hate questions like, 'Why would a father send his son to die?'"

"And you loved asking them, I bet. Ever get a satisfactory answer?"

"I've learned much here, including my tendency to be a smart ass."

"I kind of like that trait. And your aunt?"

"At thirteen, I became . . . she called it hot-headed and sent me back to Thailand. A stranger to my grandparents, they called me a mixed-up boy neither of one culture nor the other. I worked, cleaning up after elephants. They're such intelligent, caring animals. It infuriated me to see the handlers using them to destroy their own habitat, to harvest teak trees."

Kimika stilled, wonder spreading over his face. He grabbed Jasirey's hands. "I questioned my acceptance into the Protectors. But people's welfare depends on the planet's, and as your Protector, your lion, I can assist you in your destiny. I will do everything in my power not to disappoint you, lady."

Jasirey stood and embraced the sweet, idealistic boy. "I'm also here for you, Kimika," she said. *Child of my heart,* she thought.

He heard the words, believed she had spoken aloud and hugged her in gratitude.

Though Jasirey would dearly love to see such a thing, one person, even one society, could not hope to bring all the world's people together in caring for the planet.

Liu's idea of noetic science came to mind, and she wondered if the energy of like-minded people's thoughts could affect environmental decisions. Something to research for the future. For the present, she would learn how to navigate a new family and her role as Jasirey. As Master Kai said, "That was enough to begin with."

Acknowledgments

Thank you to Alex Arnot for the support, to copy editor and editorial consultant Phillis Scott for her help in whipping *The Devoted of Jasirey* into shape, to cover artist Elizabeth Lindgren for her great cover, and to my publisher and editor Marcia Gagliardi, whose professional generosity in collaborating with me every step of the way to publication made my first experience as an author truly memorable and my novel a better book.

About the Author

Bonnie Arnot loves stories about female heroes conquering new worlds or about historical places and people who can seem just as fantastical to the modern world. She lives in western Massachusetts with her husband, two sons, and two cats.

Colophon

Text for *The Devoted of Jasirey* is set in Baskerville, a serif typeface designed in 1757 by John Baskerville in Birmingham, England, and cut into metal by punchcutter John Handy. Baskerville is a transitional typeface intended as a refinement of old-style typefaces of the period, especially those of his most eminent contemporary, William Caslon.

Compared to earlier designs popular in Britain, Baskerville increased contrast between thick and thin strokes, making serifs sharper and more tapered. He also shifted the axis of rounded letters to a more vertical position. Curved strokes are more circular in shape and the characters more regular, creating a greater consistency in size and form influenced by the calligraphy Baskerville had learned and taught as a young man.

Baskerville's typefaces remain popular in book design.

Titles for *The Devoted of Jasirey* are set in Brioso Pro, a new typeface family designed in the calligraphic tradition of the Latin alphabet. Brioso displays the look of a finely penned roman and italic script, retaining the immediacy of hand lettering while having the scope and functionality of a contemporary composition family. Brioso blends the humanity of written forms with the clarity of digital design, allowing designers to set pages of refined elegance. Designed by Robert Slimbach, this energetic type family is modeled on his formal roman and italic script. In the modern calligrapher's repertoire of lettering styles, roman script is the hand that most closely mirrors the oldstyle types that we commonly use today; it is also among the most challenging styles to master. Named after the Italian word for lively, Brioso moves rhythmically across the page with an energy that is tempered by an ordered structure and lucidity of form.